Maybe if Maja unders~~...~~ estranged she was fr~~...~~ would leave her alone.

"My point is, I've had no contact with Håkon for twelve years and don't consider myself a Hagen." If she sounded bitter, then it was because she was... She hadn't done anything to deserve such bad luck. She worked hard, tried to be a good person, paid her taxes and flossed her teeth. What had she done to deserve to be slapped in the face with her past?

"But it's what *I* think that matters, Maja," Jens softly informed her, his voice both seductive and sinister. "It's what *I* want that's important."

She threw up her hands and turned to face him, frustration and fury bubbling up from her stomach into her throat. "Then tell me! Stop toying with me."

Jens stood up and came to stand in front of her, his expression implacable and his eyes unreadable. "Years ago, you promised to marry me, Maja, and that's exactly what you are going to do."

Joss Wood loves books, coffee and traveling—especially to the remote places of southern Africa and, well, anywhere. She's a wife and a mom to two young adults, and is bossed around by two cats and a dog the size of a small cow. After a career in local economic development and business, Joss writes full-time from her home in KwaZulu-Natal, South Africa.

Books by Joss Wood

Harlequin Presents

Hired for the Billionaire's Secret Son
A Nine-Month Deal with Her Husband

Cape Town Tycoons

The Nights She Spent with the CEO
The Baby Behind Their Marriage Merger

Scandals of the Le Roux Wedding

The Billionaire's One-Night Baby
The Powerful Boss She Craves
The Twin Secret She Must Reveal

Harlequin Desire

The Trouble with Little Secrets
Keep Your Enemies Close...

Visit the Author Profile page
at Harlequin.com for more titles.

The Tycoon's Diamond Demand

JOSS WOOD

HARLEQUIN®
PRESENTS™

Recycling programs
for this product may
not exist in your area.

ISBN-13: 978-1-335-59348-1

The Tycoon's Diamond Demand

Copyright © 2024 by Joss Wood

Harlequin Enterprises ULC
22 Adelaide St. West, 41st Floor
Toronto, Ontario M5H 4E3, Canada
www.Harlequin.com

Printed in Lithuania

MIX
Paper | Supporting
responsible forestry
FSC® C021394

The Tycoon's Diamond Demand

This book is dedicated to my sprint-writing partner and good friend Katherine Garbera. Lovely people make great writers and she's both! I'm lucky to have you in my life, Kathy.

PROLOGUE

No *DAMN* WAY. Jens Nilsen stared at the email's subject line on his screen, and the black letters on the white page danced in front of his eyes. Håkon Hagen…*dead*? The day before he was due to hear that Jens's hostile takeover of his company was a done deal.

What?

How?

Jens scanned the email from his in-house lawyer, trying to make sense of the devastating news. Håkon had been rushed to hospital with a suspected heart attack. He was dead on arrival. Jens didn't wonder how his lawyer acquired the confidential information so quickly but knew it was accurate. He paid the man a king's ransom to know everything about his oldest enemy and he expected nothing less than up-to-date information.

In his home office in Bergen, Jens leaned back in his office chair and placed his feet on the edge of his desk, his eyes on the screen but his focus elsewhere. He'd put in years of work, twelve to be precise, and billions of dollars, to acquire Hagen International with the sole purpose of watching Håkon squirm when he told him he now owned the company that had been in Hagen hands for generations.

How dared he take the easy way out by dying, and denying Jens his revenge?

The bastard.

Twelve years…twelve years *wasted*. Jens's feet hit the floor and he stood up, pacing the area in front of his Peder Moos desk. When he'd first met Håkon, he'd been a young fishing captain, overseeing his aunt's three-vessel trawler fleet, juggling fish quotas and the wild Arctic seas. He'd had a job he loved, a girl he was mad about, a good life… ambitious but not burning with it.

Then Håkon's daughter had left him.

He would've put Maja jilting him and the break-up video she sent him behind him, or tried to, but Håkon had made that impossible to do. Maja's father's decision to punish him for having the temerity to have an affair with his daughter/princess had ignited their more-than-a-decade-old feud.

Håkon added hardship to heartbreak, and his campaign of harassment had fired up not only Jens's anger but his ambition, and he'd waded into the fight. And he hadn't stopped swinging until he had as much power, financially, politically and economically, had as much money—he was a billionaire several times over—and as much influence as Håkon Hagen. All he'd needed, the jewel in his crown of revenge, was to watch Håkon's face when he informed him he'd acquired his company too.

But that wasn't going to happen now. And that was wholly unacceptable.

If Jens could exchange his empire based on shipping, gas and commercial fishing, his billions, just to see Håkon's reaction to knowing Jens owned Hagen International, he would. If he could drag him back from the dead to have that final confrontation, he wouldn't hesitate. Everything he'd done for years had been building up to that moment. He'd wanted to see the blood drain from Håkon's face, to know he held his future in his hands—just as Håkon had once held his.

What was he supposed to do now? Revenge was the fuel that fired him, vengeance was all that mattered. Hagen International was just a company, it had no feelings and didn't care who owned or controlled it. The only link left to the company, to the famous Norwegian family, was Maja...

Maja. The girl who'd stomped on his heart and bolted from Bergen, just a few hours before they were due to say 'I do'. The person he once would've moved mountains and parted seas for. She'd promised she'd be at the courthouse, had been prepared, she'd assured him, to endure her father's wrath to be with him. For the first time in his life, he'd felt wholly loved and valued, excited about his future, ready to trust, ready to love. Stupidly believing he wouldn't, this time, be abandoned.

What had he been thinking trusting her, anyone, with his heart and his dreams in the first place? From a young age he knew that if people could screw you over, they would.

And the need for revenge didn't die with death, it didn't fade away because Håkon was beyond his reach. He'd come this far, and he wouldn't be denied. Maja was out there, somewhere, and a still handy target for retribution.

Håkon might've waged the war, but she'd been the catalyst.

And, with Håkon gone, she was now a viable alternative target. The *only* target. Jens stopped pacing and squinted at the Hans Fredrik Gude landscape he'd purchased at auction last year. He'd outbid Håkon for the oil painting, and the auctioneers had achieved a record price for the artist in the process.

Håkon was gone, but Maja was…*somewhere.*

Jens leaned across his desk, picked up his phone and punched in a number. When his lawyer answered he issued a terse instruction. 'Find Maja Hagen. I don't know where she is, or what she's doing, but I want her found. *Today.*'

CHAPTER ONE

MAJA HAGEN'S FIRST major exhibition, and her first visit back to Norway in twelve years was going quite well...if she ignored the irritating issue of her father dying.

It was so typical of her father to cast a shadow over her first professional accomplishment. And if her thoughts were harsh, then that was because Håkon Hagen had been a harsh man. He was—*had been*—controlling, dominating and more than a little narcissistic. She'd even go as far as to say he'd been tyrannical, with a deep-seated need to keep all his soldiers, especially her, in a regimented, never-out-of-step line.

Was she sorry he was dead? She wished she could say she was, but she'd lost her father a long time ago. If she'd ever really had one. She'd had a man who provided her with a house to live in, fancy clothes and toys, and his instantly recognisable name. Love, affection and unconditional support, everything she'd needed the most, hadn't been part of Håkon's emotional landscape.

Maybe if she'd been his much-longed-for son, she might've experienced some affection from him. But she was just a reminder of her long-dead mum's inability to give him the male child to carry on the Hagen name. After her mum's death, and for the majority of her childhood, she lived with a cold, hard man who thought her presence in his life was a hassle.

Now he was dead, and she felt…nothing.

She'd seen, online, the photographs of her stepmother—Håkon had married his long-term mistress after Maja left Norway—outside the church yesterday, ready for his funeral. The funeral service had been strictly invitation only but, despite Håkon Hagen having few close friends—dictators and despots rarely did—many people had come to say goodbye to one of Europe's most influential businessmen. Despite his lawyer having her contact details in case of emergency, and him having informed her of her dad's death, she hadn't received an invitation to attend the service.

They'd had no contact for over a decade; she'd said everything she'd needed to say to her father twelve years ago and was happy to avoid the press hanging around outside the church and the cemetery. Håkon, pompous and patronising, always polarising, had made headlines one last time.

Right now, she should concentrate on her opening night. She wanted to hear the comments of the carefully curated guests, clock their reactions, and get their honest, unfiltered opinions because M J Slater never gave interviews or attended opening nights. It was just another quirk of the elusive, reclusive photographer.

Maja, dressed in a server's uniform of a white T-shirt, severe black trousers and service boots, picked up a tray of champagne glasses and slipped into the gallery of the premier arts centre situated on Rasmus Meyers allé. She moved to the side of the room and watched for reactions to her massive images hanging on the high walls of the light-filled space. This section of the famous Bergen art centre was dedicated to up-and-coming artists, a space to show-case the work of rising talents. Maja swallowed and rocked on her heels. After years of struggling, shooting portraits and weddings, she was starting to gain recognition as an 'interesting' and 'provocative' photographer. Best of all, her art was hers, wholly unconnected to her past and family name. No one knew M J Slater was, in fact, Maja Hagen, the only daughter of Norway's most powerful and influential businessman.

What would these people think if they knew she was Håkon's daughter? Would they like her work more, or judge it more harshly? If they knew she was Maja Hagen, they would either fawn over or despise it, and it would be viewed through a Håkon Hagen lens. She'd either fail dismally or be over-complimented, neither of which she wanted. M J Slater was an unknown artist, with no family baggage. Be-tween her father and Jens Nilson, Maja Hagen had trunk-loads of the stuff.

No, she wasn't going to think about Jens. Not now. Not today. Definitely not while she was in Bergen, in Norway. Coming back was hard enough without having to deal with the memories.

Maja deliberately shifted her focus back to her father. She wondered who would inherit Hagen International, the em-pire her great-grandfather started in the nineteen-twenties. Who would inherit his houses, his art, his billions? Her step-mother? It wouldn't be Maja herself. When she'd stormed out of Håkon's life, she'd given up her name, her country and any access to family money.

She didn't regret her decision. She was succeeding or

failing by her own merits, removed from her father's criticism and the influence of his name. She'd freed herself of his control, and she now lived life on her own terms.

Maja watched a young man, dressed head to toe in designer clothing, stop in front of her biggest image, an eight-by-six-foot monochrome photograph. He tipped his head to the side, and frowned, obviously unsettled by the provocative image of a ragged, dirty street child bending to pick up a discarded, but incredibly big and expensive, bouquet of roses and lilies. The juxtaposition was, she admitted, jarring.

Some people loved her work, others walked around the gallery frowning. She photographed the misunderstood and the isolated, the marginalised, people who stood on the outside looking in, and individuals who didn't quite fit in. Some hated their lives, others revelled in the freedom of not being accepted. Most just tried to get on with life, accepting the hand it dealt them, playing their cards as best they could, whether it was a ghetto in Mumbai or a luxury mansion in Dubai.

You could, as Maja knew, be as unhappy rich as you were poor. Did she put distance between herself and her subjects because she liked the concept of standing apart, because she refused to engage with people beyond a certain level of intimacy? Maybe. Probably.

Another perfectly groomed young man stepped up to look at the huge image. 'Who's this artist again?'

'M J Slater,' came the reply. 'I've never heard of him before, but Daveed Dyson told me he's someone to look out for.'

Daveed Dyson, the celebrated art critic, was talking about

JOSS WOOD 15

her? *Wow.* But why did everyone always assume M J Slater was a man? Not that she cared: as long as her identity remained a secret, they could assume she was a purple and pink spotted lizard.

'Where's he based?'

'No idea. There's no information on him.'

Scotland was her home now, Edinburgh her city. She was a UK citizen through her mum. Norway held too many bad memories, too much intense regret, guilt and pain, for her to stay.

The last time she'd been here, she'd been so young. So naïve. Initially so convinced love would triumph, that it stood a chance against financial power and influence. It didn't. Love withered when faced with wealth and power built up over generations, when it came up against someone as heartless, ruthless and controlling as her father.

Someone touched her shoulder and Maja turned to look at her frustrated business manager, Halston. She handed him a glass of champagne and ignored his scowl. He'd far prefer her to be dressed in a little black number, schmoozing and talking about her art with the very rich guests. He wasn't a fan of her need to remain incognito.

Maja looked away from Halston, pretending he was another guest. 'Did they like them? Hate them?' She didn't know...she never did. For most of her life, her father had made her feel she wasn't enough, and she still needed to feel validated and reassured. Would she ever outgrow that trait? She hoped so.

'That's why I came to find you,' Halston told her, making it look as though he were issuing an instruction to a server.

'It's a huge success, with one anonymous buyer buying your four biggest pieces earlier tonight at an exclusive preview.'

She placed a hand on her heart, relieved. 'Great. But we'll only be able to claim a hit exhibition when the art critics have posted their reviews in a week.'

'The curator is going to announce the identity of the buyer of the four images. Apparently, he's a big deal. I came to warn you not to react if you want to stay hidden,' Halston told her before moving off. Finding a tall table, she placed her tray on it and slid behind a huge flower arrangement. Nobody would notice her here...

The atmosphere in the room changed and then the crowd in front of her parted, as it would for a king or queen. And Maja tensed, electricity skittering up her spine as every neuron in her body caught fire. Someone tapped a microphone and called for the room's attention. But Maja had eyes only for the man standing next to the gallery curator, looking as remote as Bouvet Island thousands of miles away. Her body immediately reacted to his presence, turning hot, then cold.

Jens was here...

Memories, so many of them, whipped through her. His hands in her hair as he moved her head to take their kiss deeper, his big hands on her hips as she stood between him and the wheel of his fishing trawler, his chin resting on her head as they returned from the fishing grounds north of Lofoten. Sneaking him past the groundsman and the house-keeper working at her father's holiday home on the outskirts of Svolvær and up to her bedroom, where he initiated her into the delicious art of sex. She'd had a few lovers since, but none who had made her feel the way Jens had.

There were a few remnants of the young man she'd known and loved in the face of the man standing across the room. His face, ridiculously handsome with rugged features, olive skin and navy blue, almost black eyes, looked a little leaner. His hair, the deep brown of a sable's coat, was as thick as before, cut shorter to keep the waves under control. He'd been big before, always muscled—working on a fishing boat was not for the weak or puny—but he seemed taller, more powerful.

But the biggest change was in his attitude, in his posture, in the sardonic tilt of his chin.

Her eyes flew across his face, and she could find nothing of the young man who loved to make her laugh, whose eyes lightened with affection, whose mobile mouth twitched with amusement. This was a harder, tougher, icier version of the Jens she'd known…

As devastatingly attractive, a thousand times more dangerous.

She placed her hand on her heart. Had her fertile imagination conjured up his presence? She squeezed her eyes tight, then lifted her lids and blinked. Nope, Jens Nilsen hadn't disappeared, he wasn't a mirage. She took in his designer dark grey suit, the pale green shirt, his perfectly knotted tie, and the pocket handkerchief peeking out from his breast pocket. Black-framed glasses gave him an added layer of intimidation, something he didn't need.

'Ladies and gentlemen, let us welcome one of our institution's patrons, Jens Nilsen, the esteemed and pre-eminent collector of Scandinavian, particularly Norwegian, art. At a private viewing this afternoon Mr Nilsen made a bid for, and acquired, M J Slater's *Decay and Decoration* series, four images in total, for an undisclosed amount.'

Maja couldn't pull her eyes off Jens. He was a force field she couldn't resist. She drank him in, clocking his changes, noticing what remained the same. His presence was a magnet, and she couldn't disconnect...

Her art, the fact that she'd sold her work to him, that this was a successful exhibition...it all faded away. Jens, and his presence, took up all her mental space.

Maja watched, fascinated, as he tensed. Someone who didn't know him well wouldn't notice his fractionally tighter shoulders, or the slight lift of his chin. His eyes narrowed, and he reminded her of a super-predator who'd caught the scent of his prey on the wind. Maja held her breath as his eyes scanned the gallery, his dark eyes skimming the faces in the crowd. He passed over her. As she'd told Halston earlier, nobody noticed the servers...

But why did he ask for a private viewing earlier? Did he connect M J Slater with her? Was that why he'd bought her work? No, that didn't make any sense...if he knew the artist was the woman who'd jilted him via a blasé video, he'd be more likely to burn her work than buy it.

Jens had no idea why she acted the way she did, that all of her actions—*most* of her actions—had been done out of a desperate need to protect him from her father, to keep Jens off Håkon's radar. Maja had never wanted Jens to be collateral damage in the war between her and her father. Yet here he was, and the floor under her feet rocked and rolled.

Then, suddenly, Jens's head whipped back at speed, his eyes slammed into hers and Maja took a step back, the heat of his gaze pinning her feet to the floor. Of course, he'd find her; Jens's sixth sense for danger, for out-of-the-ordinary situations, had served him well when he'd pitted himself against the stormy Norwegian and Barents seas. He listened to his instincts, and as his eyes raked over her, seared through her, she knew, without a shadow of a doubt, Jens knew exactly who she was.

Fight or flight…she'd never faced this decision before. Flight won out and Maja fled.

She'd known it wouldn't be long before he found her in the small, tucked-away reception area on the second floor of the gallery. Maja turned away from the window when she heard the soft click of the door opening. The air in the room rushed out and she felt light-headed and spacy.

Maja released a low curse, unable to make sense of her now upside-down world. She'd never expected to see him again, he was part of her past. She'd spent more than a decade trying to get over him, to forget. Yet here he stood, six feet three inches of brutal intelligence, physical brawn and restrained rage. How could his effect on her still be so strong, so potent?

'Jens…' She swallowed, internally wincing at her high-pitched voice. 'What are you doing here? How did you find me?'

'Admittedly, you're a hard woman to track down, Maja,' Jens said, closing the door behind him. He crossed his arms, pushed one big shoulder into the wall next to the door and crossed his left foot over his right ankle. He reminded her of a big cat about to pounce. And she was his prey.

'I didn't *know* you were looking for me,' Maja replied,

ignoring her spluttering heart. There was no air in this room, she was finding it difficult to breathe. Maja felt her pulse inch upward and dots appear before her eyes.

No, she wasn't going to let emotion, and the past, the impact of Jens, override her common sense. She needed to pull herself together and start thinking instead of reacting. She doubted she would be able to control this situation, but she could stop acting as if she were a flapping fish he'd hooked. 'What do you want?'

His expression turned sardonic. 'Maybe just to say hello to the woman I once thought would become my wife.'

So many questions bubbled on her tongue. Did he know she was M J Slater? Why had he bought her *Decay and Decoration* series? Would he ask her why she was working as a server at this event?

His expression moved from saturnine to thoughtful. He walked across the room and picked up from the coffee table a brochure advertising her exhibition. He flicked his thumb against the edge as he looked down at the brochure. Maja, a knot in her stomach, walked over to him. She inhaled a hit of his cologne, something woody and citrusy. He smelled gorgeous but a part of her wished he still smelled of soap and the sea.

'After I heard of Håkon's death, I instructed my lawyer to track you down,' he said. 'He had no luck finding you.'

Frankly, luck was running short all around. 'I keep a low profile,' Maja hedged. 'And you just happened to be at this exhibition?'

'I've been collecting art for a few years now. Curators often reach out to me.' He smiled, but Maja shivered.

Something was off and she still felt the urge to bolt out of the door.

'I was offered, but declined, an invitation to a private viewing of M J Slater's work earlier this week. But, annoyed by the lack of progress in finding you, and in need of a distraction, I thought I'd take a look. I came in earlier, about an hour before the gallery opened tonight.'

Right. It didn't sound as though he'd connected her with the artist, thank God. Maybe this really was a coincidence, maybe he'd followed her out of the gallery simply to reconnect. But that wasn't Jens's style. He didn't do simple, and the tension in his body suggested this was more than just a *Hey, you're back!* chat. What did he want? What could he be up to? Why did he still make her heart bang against her chest? And why was panic, the mental equivalent of a herd of spooked wild horses, galloping through her?

Jens flipped over the brochure, and Maja looked down at the printed picture of one of her few framed images. She didn't like frames. She wasn't crazy about her photographs being harnessed by a border. Jens jabbed his finger at the image on the brochure and it took her some time to realise he was pointing to her tiny, but flamboyant, signature in pencil on the white matte board within the frame.

'You sign your m's with a distinctive flourish.'

Reaching into his jacket, he pulled out a slim leather wallet and flipped it open. Maja watched, rooted to the spot, as he pulled out a faded Post-It note and gently opened the small square. He held the corner between his thumb and forefinger so that she could see the writing.

Jens, I love you. I can't wait to marry you. M

And there was her distinctive 'M', the same one she used

when she signed her work. One was a carbon copy of the other, and a three-year-old could tell they were written by the same hand.

No!

No!

She'd wanted to think otherwise but he *knew*. He'd linked her with M J Slater. Jens was now the only person other than Halston who knew that connection between the ex-heiress and the rising-star photographer. Maja bit down on her lip, her eyes flying from the note to the brochure. Dammit. It was such a little slip-up, but one with huge consequences.

'I never expected you to keep that note, you're not the sentimental type.' If he'd tossed it, they wouldn't be here.

Jens's cold, furious eyes slammed into hers and she shivered at the intensity of his gaze. 'I keep it as a reminder of what a naïve fool I was.'

Maja bit down on the inside of her cheek, tasting blood. Panic, hot and uncontrollable, bubbled in her throat and made her skin prickle. This small room now felt smaller, darker.

Hello, anxiety, my old friend.

Coming back to Norway had been a bad idea.

After growing up with a father who hated her, who tried to control everything about her, she'd wanted to break free. Of his control, of his influence and the associations attached to the Hagen name. She'd vowed she'd make her way in the art world, away from the sphere of her father's influence, and for the past twelve years she'd worked hard to achieve that goal.

She'd come back to Bergen only because this exhibition

was an opportunity she couldn't miss, a launching pad into the big leagues, a way to get her name out to collectors and connoisseurs. She'd kept up her strategy of lying low, partly because she didn't want anyone digging into her past, partly because her elusiveness was her unique selling point. She avoided the media and refused all one-on-one interviews, wanting her photographs to speak for themselves.

As M J Slater she was shielded from the negative, and positive, connotations of being Håkon's daughter. She was, finally, being recognised, and maintaining her anonymity was beyond important. She'd made so many sacrifices and if she was 'outed' now, everything she'd worked so hard for would be lost. She had to persuade Jens to keep her identity a secret. But how?

'What do you want?' she asked, wincing at the anxiety in her voice.

'If it's an explanation of why I left you hanging at the courthouse, and why I sent you that video, why I ghosted you, I can do that, I owe you that,' she continued, hoping to move him off the subject of her art, the exhibition and her using a different name.

And after she apologised for leaving him and explained why, asked him to keep her secret, she could move on, and put him—and his breath-stealingly attractive face and body—in the past where he belonged.

Then she'd go back to her hotel room, call room service and order the biggest cocktail known to man.

Jens tipped his head to the side, narrowed his eyes and his smile held no warmth. Oh, God, she was in a world of trouble here.

'I'm not interested in explanations or apologies, Maja.'

She frowned, puzzled. 'Then what do you want?'

'Quite a bit actually,' he told her, his deep voice rumbling over her skin. 'Especially from you.'

CHAPTER TWO

JACKPOT!

Judging by the panic and fury in Maja's expressive eyes—a mixture of gold, green and smoky brown—Maja didn't want him, or anyone, knowing she was M J Slater. And that gave him the leverage he needed. It was the opening he'd needed, his path to revenge.

Jens raked his hand through his hair. Maja was the last Hagen standing, the only person he could target, but, for the first time in years, he didn't know exactly how he was going to get what he needed from her. Payback. Since discovering who she was just a few hours ago, and by sheer coincidence, he'd been on the back foot, not a position he felt comfortable with, not any more. He called the shots, laid out the terms, and operated from a position of strength. He'd forgotten how it felt to be indecisive, out of control.

Jens turned to look out of the small window, needing a moment to get his wayward thoughts, and jumping heart, under control. He'd told her the truth when he'd said that he'd come to this gallery as a distraction, but he'd immediately felt a connection to her work, and, even before he'd known who she was, had made an excellent offer for her four biggest, and best, images.

He'd done the deal and had been on his way out when he'd noticed her signature on the matte board of one of her few framed images. He'd stared at her signature for some time, unable to believe what his mind insisted was true, that M J Slater was Maja.

His expensive lawyers, and their investigative team, hadn't been able to trace her, and he now knew why. Had she changed her name legally or was M J Slater just a pseudonym she used for her work?

He could ask, but Maja was no longer the sweet, biddable girl he remembered.

She still wore her blonde hair the same way, long and loosely curled, and had the same leggy, slim figure.

Back then, like tonight, she wore no make-up, but then she'd never needed any. Her skin was clear, her dark eyelashes and eyebrows highlighting her fantastic green and gold eyes. Years ago, she dressed in bold colours and wore her frequently unbrushed hair in messy buns. Her fingers and clothes were always splattered with oil paint. He remembered names like Indian Orange, Viridian and Prussian Blue, and he'd laughed when she couldn't explain how it came to be on her butt cheek or on the side of her breast.

She was older now, and ten shades bolder than the girl with whom he'd spent that long-ago summer, a woman in every sense of the word. Powerful, compelling, and twice as dangerous.

Loving her had caused him untold grief and Jens knew, because he was a man who paid attention, she'd acquired polish and confidence, a smidgeon of power, in the years they'd spent apart. He was about to step into a field planted with landmines and he needed to watch his step.

Possibly every twitch, maybe even every breath he took.

After years of dealing with Håkon, he'd assumed Maja would be an easier proposition. How wrong he'd been.

Memories snapped at him, and images popped into his mind. Standing next to Aunt Jane as he watched his mum walk away with a wave and a smile, never to, in any way that mattered, return. Watching her, albeit from a distance, conquer the West End and then Broadway, hoping that after this play, that musical, another award, things would change. That in her next email—infrequent and sporadic—she'd tell him she was prepared to acknowledge him, the son she'd left behind and kept secret. He'd craved her acknowledgement and approval, and dreamed of a life where Flora would be a real mother.

Maja leaving him, wholly unexpected and completely devasting, had tossed him back into a place he'd never wanted to revisit. She'd caused long-buried emotions to slap and swipe him, scratch and claw. He'd hated her for sending him back there.

After she'd left, he'd used every bit of self-control he could muster, and gathered every last drop of his anger and fear, vowing to use them to fuel his ambition. He'd stopped believing in relationships and emotional connections and decided he didn't need anyone's approval but his own. He'd never again allow himself to feel rejected and abandoned. He'd left his childish need to be loved and validated behind.

He preferred action to wallowing in unproductive sentiment. Revenge to reconciliation.

It was simple… He couldn't make Flora acknowledge him, Håkon was dead but Maja would regret messing with him. And if she had to pay for her father's decisions, then so be it.

Sins of the fathers and all that.

Jens pushed his shoulders back, picking up and discarding possibilities on how to use Maja's secret identity to extract retribution. He knew something no one else did, that M J Slater was Maja Hagen, the daughter of Norway's most famous, now dead billionaire and that she desperately wanted to retain her anonymity. How could he use that information?

'Why haven't you been recognised?'

She lifted one slim shoulder and let it drop. 'Nobody expects a server to be Håkon's daughter or the artist. And Håkon rarely released photographs of me to the media, so I was never a household face or easily recognisable.'

She'd told him she and Håkon had a strained relationship but, judging by the bitterness in her voice, it had been a lot more troubled than he realised. Interesting.

'Why are you keeping your identity a secret?'

'Why do you think you have the right to ask me that?' she swiftly retorted. 'What I do, and how I live my life, has nothing to do with you!'

'So if I went out there and announced to the world that you are Håkon's daughter, you'd be fine with it?'

Panic, then fear, flashed in her expressive eyes, and he noticed her full body tremble. 'Don't you dare!' she whisper-shouted. 'I swear... Jens...' The little colour in her face leeched away. 'You *can't* do that.'

'Oh, you have no idea what I can and can't do, Maja,' he assured her. Because he preferred to keep his adversaries off balance, he switched subjects.

'I'm sorry about your father,' Jens stated.

Maja released a disbelieving snort. 'No, you are *not*. I've read about your feud with my father, Jensen. You probably raised a glass when you heard about his death.'

'Okay, I'm not,' he admitted.

What he did feel was cheated. By dying before Jens had time to inform him the hostile takeover of Hagen International was successful, Håkon had robbed him of his revenge. Håkon's dying had ended their feud before he knew Jens was the winner. Jens might've been ahead of the game, and might've had Håkon on the back foot, but it meant little since Håkon had left the world thinking he still retained control of his company.

And the world assumed they were still equals. He needed everyone to know he'd bested Håkon, that the promises he'd made to himself as a scared, hurt twenty-four-year-old were fulfilled.

'So, is stating inanc trivialities something you do now?' Maja asked, her voice dripping with disdain.

'If I have to.'

If it served his purpose. He'd do whatever he could, short of crossing the line into doing something that could land him in jail, to obtain the revenge he needed, the payback his pride demanded.

Maja made a show of looking at her watch. God, she was beautiful. Lovely and sexy, she sent blood coursing south and stopped the airflow to his lungs. He cocked his head, surprised at how much he desired her.

It was such a pity he was going to have to destroy her. But he'd made a vow, to himself and to his aunt, the woman who took him in because his mum couldn't be bothered to take him with her to Broadway, or anywhere, that he'd take Hagen down. Any way he could. Håkon was now beyond his reach, but Maja wasn't.

And, by God, he was going to make her pay. *Someone* had to.

He leaned his shoulder into the wall and wished he felt as relaxed as he looked. Memories of them rolling around in bed bombarded him—tangled limbs, streaking hands, gasps and groans—and he needed to banish them. Immediately. He could not afford to be distracted by the memory of great sex.

'So how was the funeral? Did you cry? How are you going to spend the many billions he left you?'

Her eyes turned a deeper gold, and Jens knew he was wading into dangerous waters. She made him feel raw and off balance, tumultuous and out of control. Like that stupid, in love, trusting kid he'd been, the one with dreams and hope. He'd been hot-headed and temperamental, but he wasn't like that any more. He sucked in a deep breath. Then another, relieved when his heart rate slowed down. He needed to be cool and collected. Precise and deliberate. *Focused.*

'I won't discuss my father with a man I haven't seen in twelve years,' Maja quietly stated.

She'd acquired polish in the intervening years. Strength and dignity.

'I won't say it was nice seeing you again, Jensen. A complete surprise, yes,' Maja said, her voice as cool as the wind that blew off the Svartisen glaciers. 'I'd appreciate it if you kept my identity as M J Slater a secret.'

She was worried he wouldn't, he could see it in her eyes.

But she wouldn't beg and he respected her for that. Maja rocked on her heels, then lifted her chin. 'Goodbye, Jensen.'

It had been a long time since someone turned their back on him, even longer since anyone walked away before he was done. He was one of the most powerful men—if not the most powerful man—in the country, on the continent, with a vast multibillion fortune at his disposal. He dated A-list celebrities, prima ballet dancers, supermodels and sports stars. Although his relationships were brief, he called the shots. Conversations, dates, and sexual encounters happened on his schedule, not someone else's.

He no longer allowed people, events or situations to unbalance him or upset him, nor did he permit people to dig under his skin. He refused to feel vulnerable or exposed. Vulnerability, mentally and emotionally, equalled weakness. Inadequacy, ineffectiveness and helplessness were not part of his emotional landscape.

Emotions ate away at his control. He didn't understand, or tolerate, them, so he never indulged in them, ever. Anger was always tempered by reason, affection by an innate inclination to distrust people and the things they said. Sex was a biological impulse, and he didn't have time to make convivial connections. The emptiness he sporadically experienced was a throwback to him once believing he needed his mum to acknowledge that he was hers, that she was proud to claim him, to feel whole. He was happy in his own company, content to be alone and he didn't need anyone to validate his existence. He knew better than to expect, or want, that.

He was overthinking this, giving it too much energy.

None of that mattered. He had what he craved, revenge, in his sights.

If Maja thought she was walking out on him again, she was wrong. That wasn't something he'd allow. It was time for him to take control of this situation.

'We're not done, Maja,' Jens said, his tone icily calm.

She stopped, and slowly turned around, frustration pulling her eyebrows together. 'There's nothing more to say, Jens.'

'You promised me an explanation about the past,' he reminded her. Not that it would change anything…he'd set his course and there would be no deviations.

Maja's mouth moved and he knew a silent curse had passed over her lips. She'd clearly hoped he'd forgotten her earlier promise. He never forgot, and he didn't forgive. They said the best revenge was to move on, to be happy, to flourish and to find inner peace.

Rubbish. Jens wanted none of that.

He looked at his watch 'But that will have to be another time. I need to get back, my absence will be noticed.'

'Don't let me stop you,' Maja muttered.

Feisty. Again, it was unexpected. 'I expect to see you at my home, the Bentzen estate, tomorrow night. Be there at six.'

Her eyes widened in shock. Was she annoyed he'd made her sound as if she were a parcel, to be directed around at his whim? Or was she surprised that he lived in the mansion once owned by her maternal grandparents?

'You own the Bentzen mansion?' she demanded.

'I do.' The estate had come on the market a few years ago and, on hearing that Håkon planned to add the estate to his property portfolio, he'd swooped in, made an excellent offer and yanked it away. Håkon had been, it was reported, incandescently furious.

He'd never planned on living there but, having recalled Maja's telling him how much she loved the sprawling nine-bedroomed house in the exclusive suburb, he'd thought he should, at the very least, inspect the property he'd purchased purely to annoy Håkon.

The tour hadn't gone as expected, and he'd fallen in love with the house, its amazing views and extensive grounds. He now spent as much time as he could in Bergen and was in the process of moving his headquarters from Oslo to this pretty city so he could live in the house full-time.

'When did you buy—?' She shook her head and pursed her lips, and Jens knew she was trying to ignore her curiosity. 'That's not important. I have no intention of seeing you again.'

'Be there or I'll walk downstairs and tell everyone you are M J Slater. It won't take the press long to join the dots. Your anonymity, which I suspect is very important to you, will instantly disappear.'

Fear and frustration tightened her mouth, and he knew he had her. He wasn't sure why flying under the radar was so essential to her and it didn't matter.

She sucked in a deep breath, shook her head and then her eyes narrowed. 'You wouldn't do that to me.'

That was where she was wrong. There was little he wouldn't do to exact his revenge. Sacrificing her identity? He'd do it if he had to and not think twice about it. But not today.

Right now, just the threat was enough.

'Be at the mansion at six,' Jens repeated, keeping his expression impassive. He knew she was looking for an argument she could use, a way to wiggle out of this situation, but she was out of options. He held all the power, and she knew it.

'Please don't tell them who I am, Jens.'

He heard the tremor in her voice and steeled himself against it. Payback was all that mattered.

'Then you know what you must do.'

Maja knew she had no choice but to meet Jens tonight. She'd spent the day trying to work out how to extricate herself, but he'd pushed her into a corner. Her only option was to make the six o'clock appointment and that was why she sat in a rental car a few yards away from that oh-so-familiar front door. She looked over the extensive gardens and sighed.

This charming brick mansion, built on three levels, was once owned by her maternal grandparents and the only place she and her mum could truly relax. They'd left Oslo on any pretext to visit Bergen and her *mormor* and *morfar*. She'd ridden her tricycle in the spacious hall, snuggled up to her grandparents on couches in the main living area and the den, and learned to swim in its incredible heated pool.

She remembered amazing views, many bedrooms, the four-car garage, and that her grandmother loved the huge solarium. The housekeeper had lived in the apartment above the garage, and Maja had spent many hours exploring the large garden. Bentzen House had been a refuge until her grandmother and mum had died in a car accident shortly before her tenth birthday. Her heartbroken grandfather had followed a few months later and the executors of the estate, of which she had been the heir, had sold Bentzen House. She still wished they hadn't.

Maja's life changed after their deaths, it became bleaker and darker as she slowly realised her uninterested father neither loved nor liked her. It didn't take her long to discover that Håkon didn't find her smart enough, pretty enough, charming enough…

In a nutshell, she wasn't the son he so desperately wanted

While she'd had a million regrets about *how* she'd left Jens—dumping him by video had been a cowardly act but one Håkon had forced her into—she didn't have a single regret about leaving Norway, striking out on her own, and leaving the Hagen legacy behind. She'd walked away from unimaginable family wealth and knew she'd make the same decision again. She was still Maja, but she wasn't a Hagen, not in any way it counted. She liked not being linked to her famous father and she'd protect her anonymity, her work and her pseudonym with everything she had.

She'd worked so hard to get to this point in her life, all her career success was hers alone, and she wasn't prepared to jeopardise her independence, artistic and emotional. Besides, she wasn't done with Bergen, she wanted to reacquaint herself with the city she'd known as a child. She wanted to spend time at the harbour, photographing the cheerful and charming houses or wandering down the narrow streets, ducking in and out of tiny, interesting independent shops.

She wanted to see more of Norway too. She wanted to get out onto the water, and was considering a cruise to

Svolvær, to experience the Arctic beauty in all its rugged splendour. Maybe when she was done with Jens, she'd do that. It would be an excellent way to recharge her depleted emotional batteries. She couldn't do that if the world knew who she was. And to stop that from happening, she needed to meet with her ex.

Maja leaned back in her seat and rubbed her damp hands on her thighs, trying to gather her courage.

She'd pulled on a lightweight thigh-length cotton jersey, and wore skinny dark jeans and high-top trainers. She'd arranged her hair into a messy bun, anchored with a few pins she'd jammed into her hair. She didn't wear any lipstick, nor did she check whether she had mascara flecks under her eyes or on her cheeks. She'd made no effort for Jens Nilsen. She would not give him the satisfaction of thinking she wanted to impress him. She didn't want him to think she cared about his opinion. She didn't. Not one little bit.

Their years apart had changed him, of that Maja had no doubt. The fine lines fanning from the corners of his eyes were deeper and his eyes were now more black than blue, hard and uncompromising. It was obvious his mouth had forgotten how to smile. Yesterday she'd sensed his every muscle was on constant high alert, ready to spring into action, to jump into a fight.

Jens was tense from the top of his expertly cut hair to his size thirteen feet. He was a champagne cork about to be released, a pressure valve about to blow. But, worst of all, he'd morphed into a man just like her father. Someone she'd always feared and frequently loathed. Hard-headed and ruthless, unyielding and relentless.

Even back then, there was a part of her that had been

a little relieved to be given an excuse to walk away from Jens. His intensity and self-confidence had intimidated her. Despite being so young, she'd known she would've been low on his list of priorities, and that she'd resent his single-minded focus on his career. It wasn't that she hadn't believed he loved her—he had, as much as he could. Twelve years ago, he'd been so like her father in too many ways that counted, and the realisation had terrified her.

And a part of her had known marrying him would be jumping from the frying pan into the fire.

But she did regret how she'd ended their relationship. She'd hurt him, embarrassed him, broken her promises to him and done it all in a callous manner. And Jens wasn't someone who'd let that slide. He wanted payback. But at what cost?

She had to meet with him and find out what he wanted. And whether she could give it to him. If she didn't, M J Slater would be outed, and the world would know she was the privileged and supposedly pampered daughter of one of the world's wealthiest men.

The career she'd worked so hard to build would be, to all intents and purposes, over.

She sighed. The over-large wooden front door opened, and Jens leaned against the doorframe, his eyes connecting with hers through the windscreen. He wore navy chinos, and an untucked grey button-down, sleeves rolled up to reveal muscular forearms and a very expensive, vintage Rolex. He looked fabulous, and she briefly wished she'd taken a little more care with her appearance.

Do try to remember that you are not trying to impress Jens Nilsen!

She watched, warily, as he walked over to her and yanked open her door. He gestured for her to get out but Maja, who could be stubborn, gripped her steering wheel and glared at him.

'You're wasting my time, Maja,' he curtly told her.

And who appointed him king of the world? 'I haven't decided whether I am coming inside or not.'

His blue gaze was uncompromising. 'You're coming inside, Maja.'

She lifted her chin. 'What makes you so sure of that?' she demanded.

'One, you don't want to run the risk of me telling the world who you are. Two, you're curious as to how far I'll go to get what I want. Three, you want to see what I've done to your grandparents' house, whether I've changed anything.'

Seriously? Could he be more arrogant if he tried? And damn him for being right. Before she could find her words, and fire them off, he stepped back and pointed to the front door. 'I'll be waiting for you inside.' He glanced at his watch. 'Don't be long, I don't have time to waste. I still have work to do tonight.'

Maja stared at his tall frame as he walked away from her. How dared he issue commands and expect her to curtsy and then obey? She didn't need to be here…she didn't want to be here. And she was done letting Jens Nilsen call the shots.

She'd start the car, go back to her hotel and take a hot shower. After a good night's sleep—or, more realistically, a night tossing and turning—she'd reassess the situation in the morning and work out a way to talk to, and deal with, her ex-lover.

Or…

Or should she go inside and get this over with? The sooner she dealt with him, the sooner she could move on. Maja bent down, picked up her bag and left the car, slamming the door shut. She stomped up to the open front door and walked into the familiar hall. It was empty of her grandmother's ornaments and her grandfather's collection of walking sticks, but the wide staircase was the same, as was the gleaming parquet flooring. Huge, modern, expensive paintings hung on its high walls.

Jens sat on the third step of the staircase, his forearms resting on his knees. 'How long has it been since you were last here?' he asked from his unconventional seat.

She rubbed the back of her neck. 'I was nine, nearly ten, when I last visited the house. Eighteen when I was last in Norway.'

His eyebrows rose, and Maja saw the doubt in his eyes. 'I didn't only walk away from you, Jens, I walked away from my father, and from being a Hagen. I reinvented myself. I went to university, got a degree, and started work. I have been supporting myself ever since.'

He looked sceptical and she couldn't blame him. Daughters of billionaires seldom walked away from a lifetime of wealth and ease, but she had. It hadn't been easy, but she hadn't taken a penny from Håkon since she left Norway. When she'd turned twenty-five, she'd inherited the proceeds from the sale of this house, and her grandparents' investments, but those first few years alone had been tough.

Maybe if she underscored how estranged she was from Håkon, Jens would leave her be. 'During my last argument with my father, I told him I didn't want anything more to do with him. Håkon didn't believe me, and his lawyer de-

livered an ultimatum on his behalf. I either apologised and
resumed my place as a Hagen, or I had to give up all claims
on him and Hagen International.'

'Håkon, always so kind and cuddly,' Jens snidely commented.

'My point is, I chose the latter, I've had no contact with
Håkon for twelve years and don't consider myself a Hagen.'
She worked hard, tried to be a good person, paid her taxes,
and flossed her teeth. What had she done to deserve to be
slapped in the face with her past?

'But it's what *I* think that matters, Maja,' Jens softly informed her, his voice both seductive and sinister. 'It's what
I want that's important.'

She threw up her hands and turned to face him, frustration and fury bubbling up from her stomach into her throat.
'Then tell me! Stop toying with me.'

Jens stood up and came to stand in front of her, his expression implacable and his eyes unreadable. 'Years ago,
you promised to marry me, Maja, and that's exactly what
you are going to do.'

CHAPTER THREE

MAJA BLINKED AS his words sank in, and then she released a small laugh. Jens had always had an offbeat and dark sense of humour that often made an appearance at wholly inappropriate times. Then she noticed his unchanged expression, his bleak and cold stare, and realised he wasn't joking. She crossed her arms across her chest and bit down on her tongue to stop herself from demanding to know why he wanted to marry her, what game he was playing, and what he'd get from it.

His motivations didn't matter because there was no way she was going to do it.

'In your dreams,' she scoffed. 'That's not going to happen. Not today, not tomorrow or any time in the future.' Maja threw up her hands, distressed. 'You can't *make* me marry you! You're not a Viking raider and I most definitely am not a prize to be claimed.'

His dark eyes remained steady on her face. His expression didn't change, and Maja swallowed. Oh, she recognised the light in his eyes, the sheer determination. She was his entire focus. He meant every word he said and when Jens said he was going to do something, in that tone of voice, with that light in his eyes, he was an unstoppable force.

Marrying her was now top of his priority list. But *why*? They hadn't seen each other for over a decade.

'I don't understand why you want to do this,' she told him, agitation causing her to speak an octave higher, her words tumbling over each other.

'You don't need to understand my motives, Maja. You just need to fall in line, which you will, because if you don't I will dismantle the life you spent the last twelve years building,' Jens told her, sounding completely assured. 'Follow me,' he said, before he turned and walked into the bigger of the three reception rooms.

Maja watched him walk away, moving silently despite being so broad and tall. In a daze, she dropped her bag onto the chair next to the hall table but her feet were glued to the floor.

Marriage? *Seriously?*

It was, genuinely, the last thing she'd expected him to say, or suggest. How could he want to marry her, the girl who'd dumped him via a blithe video twelve years ago, the daughter of his biggest rival? What was he thinking? *Was* he thinking?

Maja jammed her hands into the back pockets of her jeans and rocked on her heels. Of course he'd thought this through, Jens wasn't someone who made irrational and impulsive decisions. She didn't know his reasons for his out-there suggestion but she knew he had a plan…

He *always* had a plan.

Once, a long time ago, she'd thought marrying Jens was the be-all and end-all. It was all she'd wanted, being his wife was all she'd desired. He had been, was still, magnetic and charismatic, dizzyingly attractive. And any woman with strong instincts recognised he was the alpha male of the pack, and being his mate came with significant advantages.

But even back then, when she was alone, doubts would creep in. Away from him, she'd remember their conversations, and she'd realise that there were often times her initial plans for the day—to paint or to read or to visit with her friends—had changed because Jens wanted to do something else. And if she tried to get her way, he'd either boss her into doing what he wanted or give her the silent treatment until she changed her mind. She'd resented his inability to compromise or to see situations from her point of view.

And once she'd seen it, she couldn't stop. She'd started looking for similarities between him and her father and initially only found two—his ambition and incredible work ethic. As she'd looked, she'd found more—impatience, streaks of intolerance, and overriding self-confidence. By the time they were to marry, there had already been a part of her that craved an out.

Then Håkon had given her one. He'd given her an ultimatum. Break it off and have nothing else to do with Jens or he'd systematically and with great precision dismantle the fishing operation Jens managed for his aunt and would one day inherit. Håkon had threatened to have their fishing quotas yanked, buy out the mortgage loans and get them evicted, and poach their staff. Jens would have had to start from scratch.

Either she walked away and he'd leave Jens untouched, or stayed to watch Håkon dismantle everything Jens and his aunt had worked for.

Maja had chosen to run...

If she'd married him, then Jens would have been fighting a battle he couldn't win and she would have become a faded version of herself. Just as her mother had done; she'd withered away under Håkon's heavy hand. If she'd married Jens back then, she'd have risked her independence, her creativity, and her hard-fought battle to find herself.

If they married now, the same would happen. She could see the signs. How could she get out of this? What could she do to change his mind?

What if she just called his bluff, and walked out? What if she told him to do his worst? Well, his worst would be him revealing that she was M J Slater, and she'd lose her anonymity. Art connoisseurs and critics would look at her through a different lens, her art would be compromised. She didn't want her career to be influenced, in any way, by her connection to her father and the Hagen dynasty. She'd worked too hard to allow that to happen.

Maja paced the hall, feeling alone, scared, and cornered. Would it help if she explained why she'd dumped Jens in such a cowardly fashion? Would it help for him to know she had been trying to protect him from her father? Or would that simply anger him further? Would he believe her? Would he even care?

Maja walked into the exquisitely decorated room to join him. Because, really, she had no other option.

Jens walked over to the hidden drinks cupboard in the corner and hit a button. The door slid back, revealing ten different whiskies and every type of spirit available. The fridge under the shelves held all the mixers. It was a hell of a hidden bar. He reached for his favourite twelve-year-old whisky, tossed a bigger than normal measure into a crystal tumbler and threw it back, enjoying the warmth, then the burn.

He had a new goal, a fresh mountain to climb, a new challenge to conquer. Maja was going to marry him—just as she'd promised twelve years ago. And as she walked down the aisle in an expensive wedding gown, he'd show the world he'd bested Håkon, that he was the winner. That he had everything of his. It was the only way to get revenge and, hopefully, Håkon would flip over in his grave.

Maja in a wedding dress would complete the circle. It made sense. His wanting to be with Maja had kicked off his feud with Håkon and his declaration to marry her would be the ultimate 'up yours'. They'd become engaged and he'd insist on them marrying soon.

And then, in front of a packed church, he'd leave her at the altar, just as she'd left him all those years ago.

An eye for an eye, a tooth for a tooth...

But between now and then, he'd have to ride out a few storms.

Blackmailing Maja into marrying him and then jilting her at the altar was his only shot at getting retribution. Last night, he hadn't known how to use her secret identity as leverage, but it hadn't taken him long to figure it out.

And in six weeks, two months at the most, he'd be done with the Hagens for good. They'd be nothing more than a speck in his rear-view mirror.

Jens didn't ask Maja what she wanted to drink, he just lifted the bottle of Macallan and dumped two fingers into crystal tumblers. He carried the glasses over to where Maja stood and pushed one into her hand.

'Butler's night off?' Maja sarcastically asked.

He shrugged, not bothering to explain that there was no butler and that he only had a housekeeper come in a few times a week to clean. He sent his laundry out and had ready-made meals delivered for nights he didn't feel like cooking for himself.

As a child of privilege, she wouldn't understand he still wasn't used to his incredible wealth. That he allowed himself no time to enjoy it. He still subscribed to his aunt's ethos of purchasing only what he needed, not what he wanted. He owned this mansion because he'd bought it out of revenge, and the impressive Oslo flat because he needed to live somewhere close to his company's headquarters. He'd built a luxurious cabin on a private island to the east of Svolvær on land he'd inherited from his aunt for those times when he felt he couldn't breathe, for when it felt as if the city were closing in on him. He had a small boat for when he needed to get out onto the ocean, one car—the Range Rover outside—and a Ducati superbike for when he wanted to get somewhere fast. Or when he needed the wind in his hair and couldn't get out to his boat.

He wasn't into 'stuff', didn't have multiple houses around the world, and when he needed a private jet, or helicopter, he rented one. His only indulgence was art…paintings and sculptures, with a specific emphasis on Scandinavian art. He'd spent many hours listening to Maja about the techniques of her artistic heroes, her favourite paintings, had loved watching her paint and draw. It was the only thing that had stuck after she'd abandoned him.

Jens placed his empty glass on a side table and walked over to the huge doors, reaching up to move the bolt. The doors slid into the walls with a whisper, and he stepped out onto the terrace, immediately heading for the balustrade stopping his guests from falling into the huge heated pool below. He loved to swim—it was his favourite way, apart from sex, to relax.

Sadly, swimming was the only option on the cards tonight.

He turned his head to look back. Maja still stood in the doorway, her eyes on him. She was both puzzled and furious, and she looked exhausted. He had that effect on people. 'What exactly do you want from me, Jens? What are you planning?'

Okay, he'd tell her. Again. Maybe his message would, eventually, sink in. 'We're going to get engaged, plan a huge wedding and you're going to walk down the church aisle in a white dress.'

'So you said,' Maja retorted. 'But, for the sake of moving this conversation along, why would I do that? Why do *you* want to do that?'

'Explanations aren't going to change the outcome, Maja, so we'll skip them.'

'You're expecting me to marry you without an explanation, without some sort of rationale for your ridiculous demands?'

Basically. Jens looked away from her and into the still, fresh night. This situation was complicated and if he had any sense he'd walk away from it, close the door on the past and move on. But that wasn't an option and walking away from his chance to do to her what she did to him was too good to pass up.

He glanced at the huge hot tub at the end of the decking, wishing he could sink into the super-hot water and let the jets massage away his tension.

'I want revenge, Maja, it's that simple.' Jens turned his back to the railing. She wasn't going to let this go without an explanation, so he'd give her the edited, slightly embellished version. 'I presume you know that your father and I locked horns over the years.'

Her expression turned impatient. 'You two were engaged in a decade-long feud, Jens. I read about it, decided you were both fools and refused to read Norwegian business news again.'

She made them sound as if they were children when their fight had been deadly serious with billions of dollars at stake. 'Before Håkon died, I staged a hostile takeover of Hagen International.'

She frowned at him, wrinkling her nose. 'What does that mean? That you were going to buy it without his consent?'

'It's more complicated than that,' he explained. 'Your father was the majority shareholder of the organisation, but he wasn't the only shareholder. The company revenues were sinking, shareholders' dividends also dropped over the past few years. I bypassed your father and approached the shareholders directly and made an offer to buy them out.'

'And they were prepared to sell to you?'

'Yes, I acquircd enough shares to make me the principal shareholder. It cost me a bloody fortune, but I was in a position to force your father to dance to my tune.'

'And that was something you wanted to happen, right?'

'Absolutely,' he replied, his voice rising. He cleared his throat, cursing his lack of control.

Keep it tidy, Nilsen. Cool and calm.

She narrowed her eyes, folded her arms and tapped her foot. 'How did the feud start? Did something happen between you and Håkon after I left?'

And wasn't that the understatement of the year?

Her father had wanted to put him in his place for having the temerity to think he could marry Maja in the first place, and he had done his best to destroy him and his business. He'd threatened Jens's and his aunt's livelihoods because Jens had had the cheek to sleep with his daughter, because Jens hadn't known his blue-collared place. He wasn't going to waste the energy explaining that to Maja because, surely, she already knew how their feud had started. She had been the cause of it.

'Your father is dead, and you're here,' he stated, being deliberately cryptic.

'If I could just explain about—'

'I don't need explanations, Maja! There's no excuse for what you did, for the way you did it, so save your breath.'

Maja pushed both hands into her hair and held her head. 'Jens—'

The heat under his temper increased and he felt a bubble of frustration pop, annoyance burn. That he wanted to fight with her, to yell and shout, was a surprise. That wasn't the way he operated any more. She made him feel raw and off balance, tumultuous and out of control.

He didn't like it. At all.

Anger, disappointment and hurt swirled, begging for his heart to let them in. If he opened that door, they'd walk in and take over. Not happening. He needed to focus his attention on revenge. It was easier to handle, clear and sharp.

He gulped at the cool night air, letting it wash over him. He needed to get this done. He'd tell her what he expected to happen, what would happen. She needed to be very clear about what he expected from her.

'Some time soon, I will have to confirm I initiated a hostile takeover of Hagen's and that my takeover bid was successful. I'm going to take flak in the press. I will face accusations of pushing him too hard, that our feud led to his heart attack. That it got out of control.'

'Did it?'

He shrugged. Håkon had enjoyed their feud, far more than Jens did. If he was ruthless, then Håkon was amoral. There wasn't a line he wouldn't cross, and Jens had figured that if he was keeping the old man occupied, then some poor sucker out there was saved the ignominy of dealing with Maja's father.

'News of our engagement will negate any bad press.' Not that he cared what people thought about him and his actions. 'We'll tell everyone that, through you, Håkon and I reconciled, and that he approved of our relationship.'

'And you think people will believe that?' she demanded, radiating scepticism. 'I haven't been seen in my father's company for more than a decade, Jens.'

'When asked where you were or why you were never seen together, he always said you were determined to live your life out of the limelight, and that you wanted to keep your relationship private. And people will believe what I tell them to.'

Maja snorted. 'God, you're arrogant!' She wasn't wrong.

'And trust my father to find a smooth way to explain away my absence from his life.'

'It was a surprisingly effective strategy. Nobody, not even me, suspected you were estranged.' She'd covered her tracks well, and Jens knew Håkon's fierce pride wouldn't have let anyone suspect he and Maja had had irreconcilable differences.

'But now you're back and you're going to stay here, and plan our huge, glamorous wedding.'

She looked at him blankly for a few seconds. When his words settled, she shook her head so hard a thick hank of hair fell from her bun. 'Oh, I am so not doing any of that!' Maja sat down on the edge of a chair and then immediately sprang to her feet, vexatious energy radiating from her. 'This is ludicrous, Jens! Marry? You? I have three words… no, damn, and way.'

He'd planned for this reaction and knew how to counter her resistance. He knew her weak spot.

'That's your choice. But if you do not agree to marry me, move in here and plan the wedding, I will draft a press release and send it to every entertainment editor of every newspaper, print and online, out there. In it, I will detail our relationship, how you broke up with me, and how you left Norway and your father behind. That you were estranged for years.'

He watched as the colour left her face and wondered why he felt a little seasick. It wasn't as if she were innocent. She was the spark that had ignited the war. She had left him. She had *jilted* him. This was payback. He was entitled to it…

He pushed back his shoulders and injected steel into his spine. He needed to find some control. 'I will tell everyone M J Slater is Maja Hagen, and insinuate you used your contacts as Håkon's daughter to snag the exhibition at the gallery. I will also express regret at having purchased your images, that I believe I overpaid and that, on closer examination, your work is derivative and puerile.'

He was a respected collector and had a reputation for spotting new talent and new trends. His word was respected in art circles. A dismissive comment from him could ruin careers bigger and brighter than hers.

She was bone-white now and Jens watched as she swayed, her eyes brilliant in her marble-like face. She cared less about her past as Maja Hagen than she did about being outed as M J Slater. She wanted to protect her artistic identity and her work. Interesting.

'If you say that, about my art, I'll never sell another image again.'

He would never do that to an artist, any artist—even Maja—but she didn't need to know that. He couldn't tell her she was the best photographer he'd seen in a while, and that, on seeing her work, he'd felt the hair on the back of his neck lift. Before he'd even known who she was, he'd known she was a once-in-a-generation talent.

But she didn't need to know that. She just needed to agree to what he wanted, and what he wanted was for her to become his bride. And because he knew she'd do anything she could to protect her name and her reputation, he knew his 'yes' wasn't far off.

She held up a hand, and he noticed her trembling fingers. 'So, I either marry you or lose my career and my reputation?' she shouted, her words dancing on the wind. She put her hand to her head to hold back her messy hair and bit down hard on her bottom lip. When she released her grip, he saw teeth marks on her lower lip. Desire speared through him and he fought the urge to rush over to her and kiss those marks away.

He wanted to take her in his arms, to turn the anger in her eyes to desire, to feel her sink against him, her slim body pushing into his. The heat they'd generate would cause the paint on the walls to blister, would make the water in the pool boil.

No. Sex wasn't important, payback was. He *needed* to do this. He needed to close the circle and move on.

'Don't do this, Jens. *Please.*'

'I want to announce our engagement in the next week or so. I'll leave it to my PR department to release the news when it's guaranteed to make the most impact. We'll marry, in a glitzy, huge ceremony in six to eight weeks,' he told her. 'Which you are going to organise because I have more important things to do.'

'And how long do I have to stay married to you, or is this a life sentence?' Maja demanded, her voice shaky.

He hadn't thought that far ahead, mostly because he knew they wouldn't be getting legally hitched, as he intended to walk out on her before she got to the altar. He thought fast. 'A year,' he stated. That sounded…reasonable, he supposed.

He saw the capitulation in her eyes, in the way her shoulders slumped. Instead of feeling triumphant, he felt a little sick, and cold. Inside and out. Where was the hit of adrenalin, the rush of success? The satisfaction? He shrugged off his questions and told himself that it would come, that he'd experience satisfaction when he jilted her at the altar.

'Glitzy weddings are not organised in six weeks, Nilsen.

They take years of planning.' He lifted his eyebrows, wondering why she was arguing a minor point when they had other, bigger issues at stake.

'I just spent billions acquiring Hagen International, Maja,' he told her. 'Do you really think I couldn't get someone to plan a lavish wedding in that time if I threw money at it?'

Maja closed her eyes and clenched her fists. He'd put her in an untenable position. But she wasn't going to back down. Maja was a fighter and that was what he'd loved about her. 'I won't do it, Jens.'

'You *will* do it, Maja. You don't want the world to know who you are and if you walk out of here without agreeing to do this, I will tell them.' He paused before continuing, letting his threats sink in.

'Take the rest of the weekend to come to terms with the idea, to wrap your head around marrying me,' he added, suddenly, and strangely, tired. 'I won't announce our engagement until Monday at the earliest.' He gestured to the still-full glass she held. 'Can I get you something else to drink?'

The glass whizzed past his head, and he heard it crash on the pool deck below. It was a good thing her aim hadn't improved in the intervening years. He hoped none of the glass shards had landed in the pool itself, they'd be a problem to find in the crystal-clear water. He wiped a splatter of whisky from his cheek and sighed. That whisky was too good to waste, and the glasses had been a matched set of twelve, rare and eye-wateringly expensive.

New blotches appeared on her neck and chest, and her cheekbones turned scarlet. 'You threaten me, blackmail me, demand that I marry you and then calmly ask me what else I'd like to drink? What *else*? Why don't you ask me to sleep with you while you are at it?'

Well, that would be a phenomenal bonus. But…*no*. He was arrogant but not an idiot. He knew that, despite need and lust rolling through him, tightening the fabric of his trousers and heating his blood, despite never wanting a woman more than he wanted Maja, he couldn't let that happen.

He knew that if he slept with her, if he held her close, stroked her amazing skin and tasted her again, he'd be lost. In her, and in the sexual heat they'd always managed to generate. In having her, his need for her would grow, and that would complicate things unnecessarily when the time came to walk away from her. He needed to be able to stay dispassionate, and emotion-free. He needed to be able to leave, and sleeping with her would make that difficult, if not impossible.

But, damn, he wanted her. Seeing her standing in front of him, close enough to smell her heated skin, he burned for her.

He caught Maja's smirk and knew she was waiting for him to lose his cool and his control. He wasn't the impetuous, hot-headed boy she'd known, the one who'd been stupidly, indescribably in love with her. The man who would've done anything and everything for her. He'd craved her back then, convinced that every moment they were alone and he wasn't inside her was a lost opportunity…

He'd put all his dreams for the family he'd never had, for the acknowledgement he'd never felt, the love he'd never known, onto her and had thought she was the answer to all his prayers. Now she was the means to exact his revenge.

That was where her usefulness started and ended.

If he wanted sex, physical relief, he could easily arrange dinner and a few hours in bed with one of a handful of female friends who understood that sex didn't come with strings. Besides, sex wasn't what he wanted from Maja. No, that was a lie, he still wanted her, as much as he ever did. He wanted to wrap her hair around his fist as he nibbled his way down her throat, to her nipple, down her stomach, lower...

But sex would only complicate what was already a convoluted situation. If he took one wrong turn, one misstep, he'd lose himself in her and that wasn't something he wanted, or was prepared, to do.

He forced himself to lift a lazy eyebrow. 'I'm not interested in sleeping with you, Maja.'

Internally, Jens braced himself, waiting for the out-of-the-blue lightning bolt to nail him for that massive lie. When nothing happened, he sent a disbelieving look at the clear sky and shook his head. Maja, and her presence, were turning him from a logical, clear-thinking and practical man into an idiot.

And that was before he touched her. If they connected physically, there was no doubt she'd melt his brain. And his scruples.

'You're not my type any more.'

He thought he saw hurt flicker across her face, but it was gone too soon for him to nail it down. But her derision and annoyance were easy to see. 'Why are you acting like this, Jens?'

Because she and her father had forced him to. Because being robotic, and difficult, and emotionally detached were far less risky than opening up and letting yourself be *seen*, out of control and full of emotion. He couldn't let her get under his skin.

'You don't like being treated the way you treated me, do you?' he whipped back.

He stared at her, off balance. It had been a long time since he'd been challenged or made to work hard for anything he wanted. What he wanted was, usually, immediately granted. Nobody argued with him or pushed back.

And if he was tired, then she had to be as well. 'Go back to your hotel, Maja,' he told her, furious with himself for not keeping better control of this conversation and situation. 'We'll talk later.'

She lifted her head, and her green-gold eyes nailed him to the terrace.

He recognised the determination in her eyes and watched as she pulled in a deep breath, then another.

'You've put me in a horrible, untenable situation, Jens, and I'll never forgive you for this,' she told him, her voice full of venom.

Forgiveness wasn't something he expected.

'I'll marry you in six weeks on one condition,' Maja stated.

'You're not in a position to make—'

'Listen to me!' Maja's fierce interjection had him tipping his head to the side, surprised by her scalpel-sharp tone. 'I wish I had the guts to call your bluff, to believe that the man I knew would never do this to someone he once professed to love, but I don't recognise you any more. Or maybe I do. You've turned into my father, a ruthless, hard-hearted, selfish bastard. Merciless, iron-fisted and cold-blooded.'

They were only words, and he'd heard them before. But instead of rolling off his normally thick hide, they landed as red-hot acid drops on his skin.

'If I agree to marry you, I need your assurance that you will not tell anyone I am M J Slater,' she said, her voice croaking with fear. 'Do I have it?'

'I want the world to know you as Maja Hagen. I'm not interested in your pseudonym,' Jens told her.

'Do you,' she asked through gritted teeth, '*promise?*'

He nodded. And after a beat, Maja nodded back. So she trusted him to keep his word. Interesting. Did she know, or simply sense, that he wouldn't break his promise? He lied, and manipulated words and situations for his benefit, but he never broke a promise. His mother had made too many to him that she'd never kept, and breaking his own was a line he wouldn't cross.

The only time he would ever do that would be when he jilted Maja. He was promising to marry her, with no intention of showing up. This one, never-to-be-repeated time, his need for revenge outstripped his desire to keep his word. And he refused to analyse how he felt about that.

She slowly nodded. 'So, I'll be Maja Hagen for this sham engagement. We'll keep M J Slater out of this.'

That worked for him.

Maja cleared her throat and Jens knew there was more. 'Then I have only one more thing to ask…'

'What is it?'

'The reviews for my exhibition come out a week today.

I'd like you to delay the announcement of our engagement until after then.'

Why? What difference did it make? He lifted one eyebrow, silently asking for an explanation.

Maja ran her fingertips across her forehead, her eyes on the floor. 'You're asking for a lot, for me to upend my world, but I'm just asking for a week.' She placed her hands on her hips and lifted her left foot and placed it behind her right calf. Her top teeth bit down into her bottom lip. 'The exhibition is a big one, and my first truly major one. I worked hard to land it. It's the culmination of years of hard work.'

He was aware of how difficult it was to break into the big leagues.

'The exhibition is due to run for another month, but the art-critic reviews will be published a week today. Once they are out, my reputation will be...well, if not cemented, then a great deal more solid than it was before. It might even be able to withstand a bombshell exposé stating that M J Slater is Maja Hagen.'

'I've already said that if you agree to marry me, your secret will be safe.'

She sent him a harsh, narrow-eyed glare. 'Forgive me if I find it difficult to trust you,' Maja shot back. 'I'd like the reviews out before we get engaged. Just as a little extra insurance.'

He couldn't blame her for not trusting him at his word. 'You aren't in the position to demand anything!'

'Yet I still try.'

She was fluent in sarcasm. 'You started this,' he said, his voice barely more than a deep growl.

She nodded. 'And you're ending it, Jensen. Congratulations, you're a bigger jerk than my father.' She met his eyes, fierce and furious. 'Do we have a deal?'

He nodded.

Maja sighed. 'Brilliant,' she muttered. 'Not that you care but…'

He knew what was coming and braced himself to hear the words.

'I hate you so much right now.'

Jens watched her walk away from him. In a few weeks, she'd walk down that aisle towards him, watched by the cream of Nordic and European society. He'd catch her eye and smile. Then he'd slip away and leave her standing there. Alone, gutted and utterly confused.

Just as she'd left him…

CHAPTER FOUR

A WEEK LATER Maja left the guest suite Jens had allocated her at Bentzen House and walked down the long hallway to the staircase. She lifted the long skirt of her designer strapless red dress off the floor so she didn't trip. It had been a while since she'd donned ice-pick heels and she watched every step as she made her way down the stairs, gripping the banister tightly. At the bottom of the steps, she shook out her skirt, released a thankful sigh and adjusted the low bodice. First hurdle down, a million to go.

In about twenty minutes, Bentzen House would welcome about a hundred carefully chosen guests for a last-minute summer soirée with a surprise announcement. A string quartet was set up on the terrace, waiters would serve glasses of vintage champagne and exquisite canapés. Huge vases of flowers were everywhere, and the mansion glistened and gleamed. Only the guests, and the host, were missing.

Maja hauled in a deep breath. This would be their first outing as a couple, and tomorrow the news of their engagement would appear online and in any publication that mattered. It had been a long, nerve-racking and exhausting day...week. She'd received the reviews of her show this morning, all of which were positive and, frankly, wonderful. She was, apparently, a 'prodigious talent', had a 'sharp eye for composition', and was a 'photographer on the rise'.

Her images were emotional, sensational and deeply moving, and her show was declared a triumph. M J Slater was a roaring success...

But Maja had no one to share her success with. Halston sent her a text message of congratulations, but didn't bother with a call. Her phone remained silent the rest of the day. It was at times like these when Maja realised how lonely she was, how her secret identity kept her separate from people and friendships. No one was excited for her, she had no one to help her celebrate. She was on her own...successful, but solitary. Triumphant but a little tearful too. Her reviews were wonderful, everything she wanted, yet she didn't feel as amazing as she'd thought she would.

The moment wasn't nearly as good as she'd thought it would be.

Maja swallowed, and bit down on the inside of her lip, cursing herself for feeling maudlin. She was a professional success, the rest of her works had sold, and she was financially flush...what else could she want? Not to be married, but there was nothing she could do about that. Not for the next year, at least.

Maja looked at her reflection in the antique mirror above the hall table, barely recognising the sophisticated woman staring back at her. Hair pulled back into a sleek knot, make-up subtle but impeccable. Diamond earrings glinted. She looked like a billionaire's daughter.

Maja the photographer was gone, and who knew when she would be back? She'd also run out of time, today was her last day of living anonymously, of being free to walk the streets unrecognised, to be herself. Tonight, she'd enter the elite, luxurious world she'd thought she'd left behind. From now on, she would be hounded by the press, have cameras and phones shoved in her face, and have questions shouted at her.

Tomorrow, everything would be different. In the morning she'd meet with an event planner, hired to help organise her unwanted but over-the-top and off-the-cuff wedding. The wedding she wanted no part of.

She frowned and tapped her finger against the elegant table. Why should she get involved in any wedding preparations? Getting married wasn't what she wanted to do, so why did she have to choose the flowers and the cake and everything else? The wedding was Jens's circus, he was the ringmaster, and he could organise his own show.

Maybe she could quietly quit the wedding arrangements, doing as little as she could get away with. She had to be careful, a little sneaky, because she didn't want him to act on his threat.

She'd give as little input as possible without raising Jens's suspicions. It would be a difficult path to walk but there was no way she was going to *help* him blackmail her. Maja felt her throat close, and her breathing turn shallow... She just needed to stay married for a year. Then she could divorce Jens, slink back into obscurity, and go back to her very normal life. M J Slater wasn't an artist who did exhibition after exhibition so, after twelve or eighteen months, M J Slater could make a reappearance in carefully selected galleries.

Her career would be okay, and M J Slater, providing Jens kept his word, would remain anonymous. She'd be the shadow behind the artist for ever, basking in her alter-ego's reflected glory.

She'd been either controlled or ignored by her father for most of her life and was used to taking a back seat. But M J Slater was a creature she'd fashioned and formed. If the world discovered the link between M J Slater and Maja Hagen, she'd lose control and the world's perception of Maja Hagen would taint and tarnish M J Slater. She couldn't let that happen. She could stand in the shadows, but she was damned if her art would.

But what would it be like to be able to claim her work? To openly receive the praise and the criticism, to stand next to her work and be proud? How would that feel? Amazing? Scary? Fulfilling? But what was the point of wondering? Publicly claiming her art was an impossible dream…

Maja heard footsteps on the stairs above her head and looked around to see Jens half jogging down the stairs, looking incredible in what she knew was a designer tuxedo. The suit emphasised his wide shoulders and long legs, and he looked *GQ*-perfect. He'd brushed his hair off his face, and his stubble was neatly trimmed. He looked sophisti-cated, debonair and heat-of-the-sun hot.

Jens saw her and he abruptly braked, his eyes widening. He swallowed and rubbed the back of his neck. He started to slowly walk down the staircase, his deep blue eyes not leaving her face.

At the bottom of the stairs, he pushed his cuff back to look at another expensive watch. 'You're early,' he brusquely stated.

She shrugged, and, when his eyes dropped to her chest,

realised that the movement showed more of her cleavage than she'd intended. 'I was ready, so I came down.'

'You look amazing,' he told her, his voice gruff. His compliment was unexpected. 'Nice dress.'

'Your stylist came over ninety minutes ago, with six dresses, matching shoes and bags, a hairdryer, a straightener and a bag full of make-up and went to work.' Maja gestured to her dress. 'This is all her.'

Maja noticed the heat in his eyes and her cheeks reddened. Caught up in his admiration, she lifted her hand to straighten his tie and cursed herself.

Keep your hands off him, Maja!

But why did he always have to smell so amazingly good? Masculine but sexy, fresh and, yes, fantastic.

Keep your eye on the ball, dammit!

He was blackmailing her into doing what he wanted, but that didn't mean she had to make the process easy for him by falling into his arms. She'd be polite when she received congratulations on their engagement, but she sure as sugar had no intention of pretending she was over-the-moon happy. She was *not* going to make this situation easy for him.

The rather large fly in her wine glass was her still bubbling desire for the man. She might think he was a ruthless emotional guerrilla whose moral code was incredibly flexible, but he made her blood run hot and her stomach squirm. When he looked at her with fire in those navy eyes, when they accidentally touched, she morphed into a force field of magnetism and electricity, sparks flying from her. She wanted him...

More than she ever did before.

Jens lifted his thumb and brushed it over her jaw and Maja shivered. 'You are going to act the happy fiancée, aren't you, Maja?'

She lifted her chin. 'Is that what you expect me to do?'

'That's what I expect,' Jens replied, his voice soft but infused with determination.

'Just to be clear, tonight will also require some PDA.'

PDA? It took her a moment to work out the acronym. Right. They were going to sell their engagement with public displays of affection. Heat pooled between her legs at the thought of Jens's hand on her bare shoulder, her spine, on her lower back. If he kissed her, even lightly, she might dissolve on the spot. If he did more, she would find herself in a load of trouble...

Bed trouble. Naked trouble. Make-her-scream trouble.

Maja dropped her eyes from his and swallowed a sigh. Young Jens, six years older than her, had had way more experience than her, and he'd been an amazing lover. But Maja suspected his bedroom skills were now as sharply honed as his boardroom skills. Under his hands, she'd melt and murmur, scream and squirm, and possibly even leave burn marks on the sheets. She so wanted his hands on her body, his mouth over hers, her naked breasts pushing into his hot chest...

She wanted him. Almost as much as she didn't want to want him.

Jens looked at the open front door, where a hired-for-the-night butler stood just outside, waiting for the first of the guests. 'The guests will be arriving soon,' Jens stated, pushing his hand into the inside pocket of his tuxedo jacket. 'You'll need this.'

He thrust a classic red ring box at her, with gold detailing, and Maja's eyes shot up when she saw the familiar logo on the outside of the box. She flipped open the box and saw a square-cut, deep blue stone. It was huge and set in a delicate platinum band.

'It's a fancy vivid blue diamond, just under ten carats,' Jens informed her. 'You'll be asked.'

'Would your guests really be that rude?'

Jens nodded. 'Yes. And no, you don't know how much it cost, you didn't ask.'

She knew blue diamonds were exceedingly rare and was pretty sure the ring must have cost seven figures, and she was terrified to wear it in case something happened to it. Unfortunately, she loved it far more than she should. 'It's stunning.'

'People expect a ring,' Jens gruffly stated. 'You didn't get one the last time around.'

She hadn't expected one, had told Jens to put the money into the business or save it for their honeymoon. She hadn't needed fancy back then...she needed it less now, but a big engagement ring made a statement.

Jens plucked the ring from the box, snapped it closed and tossed it into the drawer of the hall table. Picking up her left hand, he slowly slid the ring onto her finger, and she watched his tanned fingers as he moved the diamond ring up her finger. Was he thinking about the last time he'd proposed, how she'd laughed, then cried, how his eyes had looked a little moist? How they'd made delicious love for the rest of the night? How happy they'd been?

How had it all come to this? So complicated, so chaotic.

'By the way, your reviews are amazing, Maja. Congrat-ulations.'

Her eyes flew up and she didn't pull her hand from his. 'You read them?' she asked, surprised.

'Yes,' Jens replied, looking surprised at her question. 'They raved about your sensitive portrayal of your sub-jects, said your portraits were jarring but not patronising, and everyone complimented your composition and used words like "visual games" and "carefully constructed". You are a talented photographer.'

She wanted to step closer and push her nose into his neck, to wind her arm around his neck and let him hold her tight. It had been so long since she'd been held, com-forted, complimented. Jens's words made her stomach flip over, and she was transported back to those days of ease and sunshine, when she thought nothing could kill their love. How wrong she was.

She pulled back and yanked her hand from his grip. She dropped her eyes and blinked rapidly. She didn't want him to see the emotion in her eyes.

Jens cleared his throat. 'Is something wrong?'

She folded her arms and gripped her upper arms. 'What's wrong is that I'm being blackmailed into marrying you, and I'm being shoved back into a world I hated, that I ran from. It's wrong that I have to go back to being Maja Hagen, Håkon's daughter, your fiancée.'

Her heart screamed, and her soul sighed. She was caught between the devil and the deep blue sea, and she was drowning. She wanted to go back to Edinburgh, where no one knew who she was, where she could breathe. She knew who she was in Edinburgh, knew what she was doing, and where she was going. Now there was an impenetrable fog between her and her future. And, yet again, a powerful man was directing the weather, a fact that made her both furious and frightened.

Maja heard the rumbling of a powerful engine and knew the first guests had arrived. They were out of time, and maybe that was a good thing because she didn't want to fight with Jens, not right now. She needed all her strength to get through this evening, to pretend to be happy. To smile and lie through her teeth.

Jens threaded his fingers through hers and pulled her to his side. 'Let's take it one step at a time. Getting through this evening is the first step. Tomorrow can look after itself,' he murmured. 'You do look amazing, Maja.'

Appearances were deceptive. She wore a fantastic designer dress, sported a ring that could be seen from space, and was clutching the hand of Europe's most eligible bachelor.

But Maja would give anything and everything to be eighteen again, standing at the wheel of Jens's fishing boat, the wind in her hair and Jens's arms around her, his mouth on her neck, his laughter being carried away by the wind.

There was happiness in simplicity, peace in honesty and she'd give everything she had to go back to who they were before.

Jens stood at the back of the biggest of his reception rooms and looked over the crowded room and smoothed down his black tie. He pushed back his sleeve to look at his watch. It was close to midnight, and nearly time to announce his engagement to his enemy's daughter.

Jens looked for Maja and saw she was talking to a younger couple on the far side of the room. The huge wall behind her held all four of her *Decay and Decoration* images, and they made a powerful statement. They were amazing, she was exceptionally talented, and she deserved the kudos she'd received today. But she was celebrating, if she was celebrating at all, in private. She'd hit a massive milestone today and, because she hadn't left the house, he knew she hadn't done anything special or significant.

An achievement like hers deserved to be celebrated.

Yanking a bottle of champagne from one of the many ice buckets dotted around, he moved through the room, making his way to Maja's side. He had eyes only for the woman in the cherry-red dress.

She was stunning. And, despite having been away from this ultra-sophisticated world for a long time, she was holding her own, quietly charming, effortlessly nice. But, because he knew her better than most, he caught the strain on her face when she thought no one was looking, the sadness in her eyes when she looked at her work, saw her chest rise and fall when she released a deep sigh. He knew she found these cocktail parties hard work, that, despite having been born into an aristocratic family, she frequently felt out of place. He understood that. He'd felt out of his depth on more than one occasion—sometimes it felt as if everyone spoke in code, or played a game with constantly changing rules.

He was now wealthy enough, powerful enough, to ignore the players, to make up his own rules, but Maja had been raised to be polite, to be a credit to her father and the Hagen name. Between her pretending they were a couple in love, fending off questions about their relationship, and accepting condolences on her father's death, he knew she felt overwhelmed, and was hiding it well.

She wasn't happy, and he wanted her, just for a moment or two, to feel happy, triumphant, proud, because she was an amazing artist who deserved to be lauded and praised. He was an art connoisseur, someone who greatly appreciated how much work it took to reach her level of success...and he'd want any artist to have their moment. To roll around in their success, to lap it up. Few artists got the kudos they deserved and when they did, they had the right to celebrate their achievements.

That was his story, and he was sticking to it.

Jens ignored someone wanting his attention and walked towards Maja. His fiancée...

He was engaged to Maja. *Again.*

He forced himself to remember that she was his fiancée in name only, and their relationship—if they could call their snappy interactions a relationship—was very fake and very temporary. He was here to accomplish a goal, to close the circle, to get what he needed from her. Revenge. Retribution.

Payback.

Maja's head shot up and their eyes collided. Jens stepped up to her and placed his hand on the smooth skin of her lower back and lowered his head to kiss her bare shoulder. Silky skin, head-swimming scent. Tiny sparks erupted on his spine and danced over his skin. He hadn't had such a physical reaction to a woman since...since Maja.

Jens straightened, noticed the shock in her eyes and looked at the couple in front of them. 'I'm sorry to interrupt but can I steal Maja from you for a minute?' Jens asked his guests. Not giving them a chance to answer, he steered her away and onto the terrace. Taking her hand, he led her past the band and around the corner, slipping into his study through the door he'd unlocked earlier. Leaving the light off, he took the empty champagne glass from her hand and filled it with champagne from the bottle of Dom Perignon he held. He lifted the bottle in a toast.

'Here's to your fabulous, incredible, amazing art, M J Slater,' he softly stated.

Maja stared at him, not knowing how to take his statement. 'Uh…'

He ran his hand over her shoulder, down her arm and linked his fingers in hers. Great art deserved to be celebrated and that was all he was doing. Celebrating her success, her talent. 'Close your eyes, Maja.'

'Why?' she whispered.

'Just do it.'

Jens waited until her eyes closed, and her lashes lay on her cheeks. Pulling his phone from his inner jacket pocket, he pulled up the arts section of a reputable newspaper and started to read the best parts from her many reviews. His eyes bounced between the screen and her face, and a smile lifted the corner of her mouth.

'A force to be reckoned with,' Jens ended, slipping his phone back into his pocket, his eyes on her lovely face. 'Congratulations, Maja. That's a hell of an achievement.'

She sighed and kept her eyes closed as she sipped her champagne. 'Yeah, it is. I rock. I kicked art butt today.'

A laugh rolled up and out of him and Jens felt as surprised by it as Maja looked. She'd always had the ability to keep him off balance, to knock him off course. Back then, he could be mad as hell at something, and a quip from Maja would have him laughing. He would be knee-deep in accounts, feel her hand on his back and twenty seconds later he'd have her up against a wall, kissing her.

Her eyes opened, slammed into his and lust flared in her eyes. The pulse point in her neck fluttered, her heart rate was up. So was his, and his heart was trying to punch its way out of his chest.

Neither looked away for what felt like hours, possibly years, and Jens wondered if she was remembering the nights they spent in each other's arms, laughing, loving, burning up the sheets. The chemistry between them had always been instantaneous, a connection resulting in massive sparks and fireworks.

The urge to kiss her, to lay her across his desk and strip that gorgeous gown off her body, was irresistible. As he took a step to close the gap between them, she held up her left hand and flashed her ring.

'You said that you'd make the announcement at midnight. It has to be past that,' Maja informed her, her voice shaky.

Right. He straightened his tie and hauled in some much-needed air. To buy himself some time, he glanced at his watch and raked his hand through his hair. He reached for the doorknob and opened the door.

'Jens?'

He turned to look at her and lifted his eyebrows. She lifted her empty glass. 'Thanks for…that. For celebrating with me, just a little.'

He clocked the gratitude in her eyes and wished he could've done more. Flown her to Paris and arranged to have supper in the Louvre. Taken her on a private tour through the Metropolitan Museum of Art. Money, lots of money, could get you pretty much anything you wanted.

'Ready?' he asked.

Maja shook her head, tension sliding into her. 'No. But that doesn't matter, does it?' she said, her voice low but re-signed. They were back to being adversaries. The moment had passed, and they were who they were before.

That was how it should be. Besides, revenge was so much easier to navigate than a relationship.

Jens took Maja's hand and asked the bandleader to qui-eten the crowd. When all eyes were on them, he placed his hand on Maja's hip and forced a smile onto his face. 'Ladies and gentlemen, thank you for being here tonight. I would like to announce that Maja Hagen has done me the great honour of agreeing to become my wife.'

He felt a shudder run through Maja and waited for the gasps of amazement and mutters of congratulations to set-tle down. 'We plan to be married very, very soon, so keep an eye out for your wedding invitation.' Jens picked up a glass of champagne, wished it were whisky, and turned to face Maja. He lifted the glass. 'To Maja.'

The crowd echoed his words, but Jens didn't take his eyes off her incredibly lovely face. Attraction sparked, then burned and he lowered his head to kiss her.

In the dim light, she looked up at him, desire in her eyes. 'Don't, Jens,' Maja softly begged him, her words just loud enough for him to hear.

'It's expected,' he replied, his voice raspy with need, his thumb running over the ball of her bare shoulder. Her skin was so smooth, luscious... He knew he shouldn't touch her, understood he was flirting with fire, the possible destruction of all his plans. Right now, he didn't care. He needed to feel the lick of the flames she'd created.

'Tell me you want me to kiss you,' he growled against her lips, sounding desperate. He was.

He could demand she marry him, could blackmail her and bully her into walking down the aisle, but he wouldn't take anything she wouldn't give, he would never force himself on her.

Every muscle in his body clenched as he kept his eyes on hers, watching as she wrestled with the need to taste him again, to place her hands on him. He'd been around block, more times than he cared to admit, and knew their sexual attraction was as strong as before, possibly even more potent. He wanted her more than he did before. How was that possible? Was it because back then she'd been a girl, but now she was a woman, and more beautiful for being stronger and more experienced? She'd come into her power, and he wanted to experience it.

But, despite their audience, kissing him still had to be her choice. A part of him hoped she stepped away, that she had more sense than he possessed.

He waited. Then waited some more, refusing to drop his eyes, back down or step away. She matched him stare for stare, breath for torrid breath. He was scared she'd back away, scared she wouldn't. He lifted one eyebrow in a silent dare and watched the sparks in her eyes turn into flames. She narrowed her eyes, placed her hands on his chest and stood on her toes to reach his mouth…

Closer, closer…

And then her lips met his and he was lost. Or found. Unable to wait for another second to have his hands on her, he slid his hand over her lower back and pulled her into him, and he tasted her groan. He slid his tongue into her open mouth and when it touched hers, he felt her stiffen. It could go either way, she could either pull back or she could dive into the kiss. The odds were fairly even.

Her hands snaked up his arms, gripped his biceps and she twisted her tongue around his and all the blood in his system gushed from his head. The only thing he could do was to gather her close, as close as they could get, her hard nipples pushing into his chest, his thigh between hers, one hand in her hair, the other flat between her shoulder blades keeping her in place. Tongues tangled and duelled, slid, and Jens sighed, unable to believe he had his longest fantasy, his biggest wish, his favourite regret, back in his arms.

Kissing Maja was heaven and hell, the best of both, and everything in between. When they kissed, when they touched, everything between them—fathers and feuds— fell away and became irrelevant. All that mattered was the way they made each other feel...

Jens moved his hand so that both hands held her head, moving her so that he could deepen their kiss. Without warning she jerked back, putting space between them. 'I think we've given everyone enough of a show,' she said, keeping her voice low.

Then Jens realised everyone was watching them, some laughing, some sniggering. On the plus side, their kiss would go a long way to show his colleagues and contemporaries he'd claimed Håkon's daughter, that he was the winner in their long-standing feud. But why didn't it feel as satisfying as he'd imagined? As good as he'd thought it would feel? He shrugged it off. He was just tired, sick of people, and he had a headache.

And as the crowd surged forward to offer their congratulations, he knew he'd feel better in the morning, be back to feeling like himself. He was in control.

Much later, Maja returned from the bathroom and slipped into the highly decorated room, heaving with the great and good of Norwegian society. Her nose itched from the competing perfumes and colognes, and her head felt as if it were about to split apart. Spots danced in front of her eyes, and she wished she could go home...

Back to Edinburgh, back to where everything made sense.

Maja moved along the back wall of the room towards the open doors and stepped outside, grateful for the crisp air. Moving down the balcony, she turned the corner and leaned her back against the wall and closed her eyes.

She'd been catapulted back into her father's A-lister world, had her cheeks kissed fifty times and thanked people for their murmurs of sympathy. She'd ducked questions about why she hadn't attended Håkon's funeral, telling them she'd had a migraine on that morning and said her private goodbyes later in the day, and explained that she'd been living a quiet life out of the media spotlight.

She'd thanked people for their congratulations on their engagement, repeating Jens's story that they'd met a few months back, and it was a whirlwind romance. Unified by their love for Maja, Jens and Håkon had agreed to a ceasefire, and they were gutted a heart attack took Håkon before he could walk Maja down the aisle.

He'd lied, she'd lied, they'd both ducked and weaved.
And she was exhausted and sick to her soul. After growing up under the shadow of Håkon's narcissistic personality, she wanted to live in sunshine, in honesty. But Jens,
their past and his feud with Håkon had yanked her back
into the murkiness that always accompanied the need for
control and power.

Maja gripped the railing and dropped her head, staring
at the immaculate garden below. She was a pawn on Jens's
chessboard, just as she'd been on Håkon's. She was here
because Jens decreed it. After all, he had power and wealth
and possessed a secret he could brandish like a sword.

And she'd kissed him. Worse, she'd liked—no, *loved*
it! She'd loved every second of being in Jens's arms again,
adored the contrast of her soft body against his hard muscles, how his gliding hands and clever mouth made her
forget that he was using her, that he was blackmailing her
into marriage.

If it weren't for the career she'd worked so hard at, the
name she'd made for herself, she'd tell him what to do with
himself and where to go. But she had too much to lose...

So what could she do? There *had* to be something.

Maja bit down on her lip, forcing her aching head to
think.

She could...well, she could make this situation as hard
as possible for him. She could ramp up her level of uninterest. After tonight, she would make life very difficult for
Jens. He might want a bride, but he'd have to drag her up
the aisle by her hair.

She would not lift a finger to help him and refused to
make the process easy for him. She'd keep her distance,

mentally and emotionally, especially physically as she was so very attracted to him. He'd soon realise he'd bitten off more than he could chew.

She'd planned on slow-walking through her wedding preparations, but she was upping that to outright passive resistance. She wouldn't engage, talk to him or offer her opinion. On any subject, at any time. Jens, a man of action, someone who preferred arguments to silence, would hate every minute of her passive, robotic stance. And she was counting on him cracking before she did.

CHAPTER FIVE

'I WOULDN'T NORMALLY bother you with this, Mr Nilsen, but I'm not making any progress with Ms Hagen.'

In his penthouse office in Oslo, Jens glanced at his computer screen, annoyed at being interrupted by the video call. Especially by the wedding planner. He had a multibillion-dollar empire to run, he didn't have the time, or interest, to talk about flowers and food.

Jens sat up straight and gave his full attention to his caller. 'What do you mean you're not making any progress?'

'I've had a few meetings with Ms Hagen, but I cannot get her to make a decision about anything,' Hilda told him. 'You might be paying me exceptionally well to organise a wedding in just a few weeks, but I'm not a miracle worker and I can't get anything done without input. I was wondering if *you* could give me directions on the flowers, the cake, and the type of music you want. We're running out of time.'

No, he damn well couldn't! 'Is Maja meeting with you?' He snapped out the question.

'Yes, but she can't make up her mind. She often says she needs to talk to you before she gives me an answer. She promises to email but never does. We are no further along than I was when you first retained my services.'

Which he'd secured with a high six-figure deposit.

What was going on? Two weeks had passed since their engagement party, but it sounded as though his very expensive wedding planner was working with a ghost. Or a zombie. He told Hilda he'd get back to her and swung his feet up onto the corner of the desk, his irritation rising. He didn't discount Hilda's words because whenever he raised the issue of their wedding with Maja, she handed him a blank stare and shut down. He asked for her opinion and got no reply, he mentioned the list of tasks they needed to accomplish, and she shrugged, uninterested.

Being ignored, dismissed and not having his orders followed was an unusual situation for Jens. He was used to people doing what he demanded. A man in his position never had to ask twice—what he wanted was what happened.

Yet the wedding planner was stymied because Maja was being, at best, uncooperative. At worst, she was quietly sabotaging his plans. The part of him that wasn't furious admired her for her courage. There weren't many people who had the guts to defy him.

Jens rolled his fountain pen between his fingers, aggravated. He understood that being blackmailed into getting married wasn't the best way to inspire someone to plan a wedding, but when he'd stumbled on his path to exact revenge, he hadn't factored in Maja's unwillingness to take part in the preparations.

He should've. He usually considered all the angles and imagined all possible outcomes. Annoyingly, Maja falling back into his life had short-circuited some of his synapses. He was trying to run his company, was deciding what to do with Hagen International. There was a possibility the company could be immensely profitable with some restructuring. But he'd lie awake at night reliving their limb-melting, searing, devastating-to-his-control kiss.

Her lips had been so soft, her body so yielding, it fitted perfectly into his...

The strident beep of his phone pulled him out of his favourite fantasy and Jens killed the reminder for his about-to-start meeting.

Standing up, he reached for his jacket and walked out of his office, briefly stopping at his assistant's desk. He issued a series of orders to cancel all meetings, hold his calls, order a helicopter to fly him to Bergen. Two hours later he was parking the SUV he left at a local airport in the garage of his mansion in Bergen.

He and Maja needed to have a conversation, *immediately*.

Jamming his phone into the pocket of his suit trousers, he shrugged out of his jacket and left it on the passenger seat. He didn't bother going into the house. He had a good idea where Maja was. Tucked away into the bottom corner of the estate, surrounded by tall trees, was an art studio built by Maja's grandfather for her grandmother. The previous owner had left it as it was, and the last time he'd checked, it had been filled with easels and paints, as if Maja's grandmother had just walked out, planning to return. Maja, as she'd told him years ago, had spent many hours in the light-filled room, drawing, painting and sculpting. It was where her love of art was born and nurtured.

He'd bet his fortune he'd find her there.

He was right. She sat curled up in the corner of the couch, flicking through one of the many art books lying around. Jens noticed an unfinished canvas on the easel and the smell of turpentine hung in the air. And Maja's fingers were streaked with paint of the same colours as those on the canvas. So she'd started painting again. Interesting.

She didn't look surprised to see him and gestured to the canvas. 'Pretty awful, right?'

He could see that she was out of practice, but she still retained some level of skill. It was far better than he could do, ever. But he wasn't here to talk about her art.

'Maybe you should be giving your attention to our wedding, not to your rusty painting skills,' he coldly suggested.

'Ah.' She pursed her lips. 'I was wondering when Hilda would call you.'

He slid his hands into the pockets of his trousers, wishing she didn't look so fresh, so effortlessly sexy. This would be so much easier if he weren't so attracted to her. 'What's going on, Maja? Why can't she get a straight answer from you?'

'I can't make up my mind,' Maja told him, her eyes on the pages of the book resting in her lap. Yes, she looked amazing in her skinny jeans and patterned top, but she'd lost a little weight, and her cheeks looked a little thinner than they were a few weeks back. Her skin was pale, and she'd started biting her lower lip.

She was under mental strain. So, he very reluctantly admitted, was he. This was far more difficult than he'd expected it to be.

Every night he went to bed thinking that, in the morning, he'd be strong enough to let go of the past, to move on and that he'd release her from their engagement—his blackmail attempt—and he'd let her go on her way. But every morning, after spending the night tossing and turning and wishing she were next to him, under him—naked and moaning his name—he woke up and realised that he couldn't let her, or his need for revenge, go.

He wasn't ready to move on, not yet. Not until he'd left her at the altar, turned his back on her, and walked away. Not until he got retribution.

He needed to *win*. But winning was costing them more than he'd bargained for. She was obviously deeply unhappy. Strangely, so was he. He couldn't work out why. This was what he *wanted*.

He needed to get out of his head and focus on the problem. 'I am paying Hilda a king's ransom to organise a huge, glamorous society wedding at short notice, Maja!'

She sent him an 'I so don't care' look before flipping a page in the book. 'I know, and, because everything is so expensive, I don't want to make the wrong choice.'

Jens walked over to her, picked the book up and tossed it onto the cushion next to her. 'That's nonsense! You know exactly what you want! You are a creative person, money isn't an object, so this shouldn't be a problem for you.'

Maja looked past his shoulder, and he sighed. He didn't have time for this. 'I'm going to call Hilda, get her over here and we can thrash this out,' Jens told her.

'Have your meeting without me,' Maja said in a flat voice. 'You're the one who wants to get married, you can have what you want.'

'You're not making this easy, Maja!'

What a ridiculous statement! He was blackmailing her, why should he make it easy for her? But then why should she want to organise the society wedding he so badly wanted? If the shoe were on the other foot, he wouldn't help her to tie the noose around his neck either.

He gripped the bridge of his nose and sighed. They had five hundred people saving the date, the pre-wedding invitations had been sent and RSVPs were rolling in, but nowhere to stage the wedding, nothing to feed their guests and no cake to cut.

Not that he was going to be around to see all that. By the time any guests arrived at the wedding reception he would be heading for the South of France. Or the Amalfi coast. Or somewhere…

'I need you to drop this, Jens.'

That wasn't going to happen. He wasn't done with her yet, hadn't got what he needed from her. This was his one chance to come out on top. To get what *he* wanted. He'd tried to get Flora to acknowledge him as her son, he'd been at war with Maja's father for over a decade, Maja had already left him once. This was his chance to triumph over the Hagens. And he would. He would not be the one left to pick up the pieces. Failure was not an option.

'You've taken away my stable, normal life and my career. You've upended my life, and I don't know what the future holds. Have you any idea how that feels?' she cried. 'I feel completely disorientated.'

Of course, he knew how she felt, it was exactly how he had when she'd left. Alone, bewildered, slapped by the events, and not knowing where to turn or what to do. But he'd also been heartbroken, and unable to speak to anyone, not his co-workers and friends, because Maja made him promise to keep their affair a secret. They had been friends in public, lovers only when they'd been alone. No one knew that she'd once held his heart in her hands.

He'd been forced to nurse his confusion and pain in silence, just as he had when his mother left and never looked back. With the added frustration of dealing with her father, who'd decided to punish him for the temerity to have an affair with his daughter. He'd lost crew members he'd thought were loyal when Håkon offered to pay them triple and every time he'd tried to employ a new deckhand, the person in question suddenly got a better offer from Hagen International. Suppliers stopped ordering from him, his fishing quotas had been revoked, reinstated, rinse and repeat.

After his aunt's death a year after Maja left, the gloves had come off and his vague threat to take Håkon down became a vow and a promise. He'd sworn he'd show Håkon, Maja and the world that he was a force to be reckoned with, that he couldn't be pushed around. He'd refused to stand in the shadows any longer, and when he'd stepped out, he'd come out swinging.

He'd started by remortgaging the trawlers and taken a gamble by investing in an innovative, mostly automated fish processing plant, and the returns on that venture had been more than he'd imagined. He'd rolled that money into more lucrative ventures, bought more trawlers, and then tossed some money at a start-up gas-exploration company with new tech. They'd sold that company for a ridiculous sum, and he'd directed all his energies into becoming big enough to take Håkon down.

And he'd succeeded. Only the world would never know. Because Håkon had taken that from him too.

Tired, annoyed and irritable because his plans were skidding off the runway, Jens sat down on the high stool next to the door and rested his feet on the crossbar and studied his reluctant fiancée. Maja was a shadow of the girl he'd laughed and loved with and held little resemblance to the vibrant woman he'd met in the gallery ten days ago. It seemed as if the idea of marrying him had sucked every ounce of vitality from her and she was simply going through the motions, doing the bare minimum of what she had to do.

Jens looked down, his eyes on the intricate patterns of the old carpet below his feet.

He hadn't given a moment's thought to what would occur between Point A—her agreeing to marry him— and Point B—walking away from her when the priest asked him whether he took her as his wife. In all his planning, he'd never considered Maja's lack of cooperation, or how frustrating her lack of interest would be. That he'd have to deal with a woman who barely listened to him, and rarely responded.

And honestly, looking at her now, he was also a little worried about her. He didn't think she was eating, and, judging by the dark circles under her eyes, she definitely wasn't sleeping. But most perturbing of all, she'd stopped fighting, engaging or interacting with him. But he was too far down the road to turn around and retrace his steps. He could only go forward. Stick to the plan and see it out. He had to show the world he was good enough to do battle with the revered Hagen family. He wanted the world, and his mother, to know that he was successful and acceptable enough for Maja's name to be linked with his.

Their gazes met and in her eyes, he saw her plea to be released. She looked dejected and frustrated.

It was an accurate summation of their stalemate. But he wasn't prepared to spend the next few weeks like that. He was already frustrated enough. He wanted Maja and not being able to have her was messing with his head. He lay awake at night and turned and burned. It was a minor miracle that he'd yet to set this house on fire. If he laid his hands on Maja, he gave his house ten minutes before it went up in flames.

The heat they'd generate would be impossible to control. And that was why he'd kept his distance, moved back to Oslo…he didn't trust himself whenever he came within five feet of her. Even just sitting here in this dusty room, her lovely, light scent rolling over him, he found it hard to control his impulse to take her in his arms, kiss her madly and take her to bed.

That won't solve anything. In fact, it will make matters much worse.

He hadn't accumulated his wealth and power by being clueless, and when he faced an obstacle he couldn't climb over, he found another way around it. He needed to pivot, to find another way to achieve his goal. But what? And how?

He was a smart guy and he needed to figure it out.

Maja lifted her feet onto the old couch and wrapped her arms around her knees, tipping her head back to look at Jens. He'd been in Oslo the past few days and she hadn't expected him back in Bergen for a few more. She'd been enjoying exploring the Bentzen estate on her own, remembering her mum and grandparents. This house was a link to them and her past, but it wasn't hers. She just got to enjoy it for a short time, the only perk of this crazy arrangement between her and Jens.

A very annoyed and unhappy Jens. She'd realised that Hilda was running out of patience, but she hadn't thought she would go running to Jens for at least another week. Damn.

'How do we move forward, Maja?'

She turned her head to look at him and caught the too-brief flash of emotion in his eyes. Was Jens having some regrets or was that her imagination? 'It isn't my job to make the process easy for you, Jens.' She pointed a finger at him, then at herself. 'You blackmailer, me victim.'

Another flash of regret, this time tinged with frustration and, maybe, sympathy. Maja focused her attention on his non-verbal cues. Was he wavering? If he was, how could she exploit his momentary hesitation? She knew his indecision wouldn't last long.

Jens wasn't one to back down from a fight and arguing with him would put his back up. Maybe, instead of being bolshy, if she told him how she was feeling, she could find the empathetic, sometimes even sensitive, frequently thoughtful man she fell in love with. She could only try.

'This situation is hard for me, Jens,' she told him, allowing him to hear the emotion in her voice. 'Not only am I living in the house that has a thousand memories of the people I loved most, the people whose death rearranged my world and my psyche, but I also have to plan a wedding I never wanted. I know we planned to get married in court, but you promised we'd have a proper wedding later. I wanted small, lovely, romantic…*easy*. This wedding is the exact opposite.'

'We could've had that wedding if you didn't bail on me, Maja.'

Maja's fingertips massaged her forehead. 'I *know*, Jens! Please don't think I'm oblivious to what I sacrificed. I understand what I gave up. I think about it every day.' She'd walked away from love, from the only man she'd ever loved, before and since. She'd done it for the best reasons, but it still hurt.

Maja hadn't planned on saying that much and expected him to blast her, but his expression turned thoughtful. He nodded. Was he agreeing with her? Was that a nod to say he'd experienced the same emotions? Why couldn't he give her more? He was the most elusive, aloof and reticent man she'd ever met. Would it kill him to engage with her a little more?

Would it help to tell him why she'd left, that she'd been trying, as best she could, to protect him from her father's narcissistic wrath? It couldn't hurt. She twisted her left wrist in her right hand, trying to find the words to explain. Maybe if she did, he'd shift off his marriage-for-revenge idea.

It was worth a try. 'Can we talk about—?'

'Unless you are going to tell me that you're going to work with Hilda, I'm not interested!' he snapped, his words bullet-fast and equally painful. His eyes iced over, and his expression hardened. There was no reaching him now.

'This is your last warning, Maja. Either get with the programme, or I'll issue a press release stating that the engagement is off and I'll reveal you are M J Slater.'

Maja pushed the balls of her hands into her eye sockets, pushing back her tears. He wasn't budging, had no intention of letting this go. Like her father, once he decided on a course of action, no matter how destructive it was, he couldn't be shifted. She was trapped with no way out.

Maja couldn't give up her anonymity, so she had no choice but to organise the wedding and marry him. A year…it was just a year. Twelve months, three hundred and sixty-five days. It would go by in the blink of an eye…

You can do this. You have no choice, Maja.

Maja forced herself to look at Jens, annoyed by him scrolling through his phone. As if sensing her eyes on him, he looked up. 'We need to get back to the house immediately.'

Arrogant much? 'Why, what's the rush?' Maja asked, not moving from her seat. Jens held out a hand for her to take, but she ignored it and stood up.

He gestured to the door and stood back to let her leave the studio first. 'Hilda copied me in on an email she sent to you. She wants you to meet her at a hotel that might, for the right price, consider hosting our wedding a month from now. She's sending a car to collect you in an hour.'

Maja shook her head. 'You go—' She saw his frown and sighed. She had to be cooperative if she wanted to have any hope of going back to the life that she'd created for herself. Part of her considered calling Jens's bluff and sending out that press release herself.

But she wouldn't, because M J Slater was her creation, something completely apart from her identity as a Hagen, untouched by preconceived perceptions. Her art was judged completely on its merits. She liked it that way. Didn't she? Sure, she'd thought about how nice it would be to be publicly acknowledged, to claim her work, but she wasn't ready for M J Slater to be burdened by Maja Hagen's baggage.

Jens shortened his stride as they walked back to the house. They passed the pool and climbed the stairs to reach the terrace. At the French doors leading into the main reception room, he stopped.

'Fighting with you is exhausting, Maja.'

'I'm tired too,' Maja admitted, feeling deflated. She wasn't eating properly and hadn't had a full night's sleep since she'd met Jens. She felt as if she were living on fresh air and emotion.

'I wish we could go back to being Jens and Maja, sailor and painter,' she said, her words soft. She wanted to recapture, if they could, those halcyon days they'd spent twelve summers ago before the furnace of life had remodelled them.

'But we can't. What's done is done, and our choices have brought us here.'

'We can change our minds, Jens, we can make different choices,' she insisted.

He looked tempted, just for a minute, but then determination firmed his mouth and cooled his eyes. 'I've got to do this, Maja.'

He stepped away, and Maja wanted to grab him and shake him and tell him he didn't, that things could be different. But nothing she'd said or done so far had shifted his perceptions. Or not enough to persuade him to alter his plans.

She wasn't getting anywhere…and worse, she was running out of options.

Jens stopped and turned back to look at her. He held her

eyes as the temperature in the room rose and the air became thinner. Her eyes darted to his mouth, and she pulled her bottom lip between her teeth, biting down. She wanted him to kiss that slight sting away.

When she met his eyes again, he looked unembarrassed at the display of his desire, and she knew he wanted her as much as she did him. In every way a man wanted a woman. In every position possible.

Maja wasn't sure who broke their hot stare, her or him, but she knew that if it had lasted one second longer, there was no telling what could have happened.

CHAPTER SIX

IT HAD BEEN years since he'd visited Ålesund, and this was Jens's first visit to the Hotel Daniel-Jean, situated a little outside the picturesque town that was the gateway to the famous Geirangerfjord and Hjørundfjord. This hotel was only a few years old, originally a luxurious mansion owned by the matriarch of the historic, and wealthy Solberg dynasty. An extensive renovation, the addition of two wings and the conversion of the outdoor buildings and stables into luxurious suites and a spa earned the hotel excellent ratings and a fierce reputation for high standards and uncompromising luxury. From the passenger seat of the helicopter, Jens noticed lush lawns running down to the rocky beach of the fjord. A large jetty ended with a pretty gazebo, perfect for wedding ceremonies.

With the Sunnmøre mountain range looming over the crystal-blue waters of the fjord and the hotel able to handle a large reception for discerning guests, he was already impressed.

Fifteen minutes later, Jens sat at the hotel bar, with a good view of anyone entering the hotel lobby, a beer in front of him. He looked at his watch. He'd had his assistant check with Hilda's and was informed Maja and the wed-

ding planner caught the two o'clock flight from Bergen to
Ålesund. Travelling by helicopter was quicker and he'd bypassed Ålesund airport by landing on the hotel's helipad.
He reckoned his fiancée and his wedding planner would
arrive in half an hour, maybe a little less.

He was still surprised at his impulsive decision to join
them. In Bergen, he'd watched Maja unenthusiastically
greeting Hilda from his study window. She'd reluctantly
tossed her overnight bag into the boot of the wedding planner's car, before slipping into the passenger seat of the huge
Mercedes. And as they'd driven away, he'd wished he were
going with her.

Then he'd realised he could, and should, and would.
And as he'd packed an overnight bag and sent instructions
to his helicopter pilot to file a flight plan to Ålesund, he'd
assured himself he was following her to Ålesund, check-
ing on the hotel to make sure that his orders were being
followed, his demands being met.

He was gatecrashing their hotel inspection because he
wanted to get this wedding business done and dusted—he
hated loose ends. It wasn't because Maja was Maja and
wherever she was he wanted to be. He wasn't a pining,
driven-by-hormones teenager, for the love of God!

No, he wasn't twenty-four any more, and naïve, and
his happiness didn't, and never would again, depend on a
woman. Maja had crawled under his skin twelve years ago
but now he had an impenetrable exoskeleton. He'd been
burned once, he'd never become emotionally entangled
with anyone, much less Maja Hagen, again.

When he left Maja standing at the altar, he'd close the

book on this part of his life and start a new chapter. He'd never think about his mum again, forget that Maja left him with a breezy, vague explanation, and that her father stomped all over his life.

It would all be *over*...done.

Jens took a big sip of his beer and remembered her attempt to explain, yet again, why she did what she did. He'd closed her down, not wanting to hear what she had to say. Was that because he was afraid she had a vaguely good reason for her actions and because he might be tempted to forgive her? And if he forgave her, would he lose his reason for revenge?

No, he'd shut her down because an explanation now couldn't, wouldn't change a damn thing, including his mind. Maja was the only one left who could give him what he needed, what he deserved.

Some might say he was taking things too far. He didn't see it that way. He saw it as evening the score.

'I always thought that Ålesund was the perfect setting for a fairy tale, and the hotel is stunning. From what I've seen so far, and if it can handle the volume of guests, I'm sure your fiancé would agree it's a suitable venue for the wedding.'

Jens looked around to see Maja and Hilda walking into the wood-panelled bar. Maja wore a soft white T-shirt tucked into steel-grey wide-legged trousers. Her hair was pulled back into a loose bun at the back of her head.

'We'll see,' Maja coolly replied, her left hand holding the strap of her tote bag. Blue fire flashed from the diamond he'd placed on her finger. It looked good on her. He desperately wanted an opportunity to see her when his ring was *all* she wore.

He shifted in his seat, uncomfortable in his suddenly tighter trousers.

'We have a meeting with the hotel manager in half an hour,' stated Hilda—small, elegant, a little fierce. 'I think it's the perfect venue, elegant and upmarket, frankly magnificent. I love its grey slate roof, bright white walls and blue trim. It's a very romantic setting.'

Maja, who still hadn't noticed him, looked out of the huge, round bay window, taking in the amazing view of the mountains looming over the fjord. 'Man, that view grabs me by the heart and won't let go,' she murmured, pulling out a chair at one of the round tables close to the window. 'Do we have time for a coffee... *Jens?*'

He half smiled at the shock on her face. He lifted his beer in a mock toast, slid off his seat and walked over to them. Ignoring Hilda, he dropped a kiss on her temple, and left his lips there, enjoying her scent and smooth skin. When he eventually pulled back, he clocked the confusion in her eyes at his public display of affection.

'My schedule opened up and I decided to join you,' he explained, keeping his tone bland.

She narrowed her eyes at him, instantly suspicious. Smart girl. Jens sent her an enigmatic smile and turned to greet Hilda. He explained his arrival and expressed his approval of the hotel. 'I'd like to see more before we say yes,' he told Hilda. 'But it looks promising.'

'It's a long way from Bergen,' Maja said, reluctant, as

always, to give an inch. 'Can we expect people to go so far out of their way to attend a last-minute wedding?'

'Dear girl, the guests at your wedding are wealthy beyond meaning, and if they don't own a plane, they will charter one to get here. Come now, you're a Hagen, you should know this.'

Jens didn't have a problem crossing swords with Maja, but he was damned if he'd let anyone patronise her. He placed his hand on Maja's back, handing Hilda his most intimidating glare. She, like many before her, instantly deflated. 'Why don't you meet with the hotel manager while my fiancée and I explore the hotel?' he suggested.

It wasn't a request and Hilda was smart enough to understand that. She nodded and with a small, apologetic smile, bustled off.

Jens pulled the chair out for Maja. 'Do you still want coffee, or would you prefer something stronger? A glass of wine? A cocktail?' He glanced at Hilda, glad to see the back of her. 'A bat to whack her with?'

Maja flashed a quick smile and his stomach flipped over. 'She's hard work. Can you see why I don't like spending much time with her?'

He knew she was angling for a way to get out of the wedding preparations, but he wasn't going to give her one. 'You're her client, don't let her speak to you that way. What do you want to drink?'

She ordered an Irish coffee and placed her elbow on the table, her chin in her hand, her eyes on the stunning vista outside.

'When last were you in Ålesund?' Jens asked, taking the seat opposite her and stretching out his long legs. He had a gorgeous view in front of him, and an even lovelier woman next to him. His phone was off, and he was, currently, unreachable. He felt the tension in his shoulder muscles ease, and his jaw loosen as he relaxed.

The world wouldn't stop if he did nothing for a minute or two.

Maja looked at him, the butterflies in her stomach on high alert. With his broad shoulders, aviator sunglasses hooked into his shirt and wind-tousled hair, he looked like an advert for a very expensive men's cologne. She'd been surprised to see him here, then not surprised at all. Jens was too much of a control freak to let something as important to him as their wedding be in someone else's control. When it was important, Jens liked to get his hands dirty.

She saw the tilt of his head and remembered his question about Ålesund. 'Oh, I was a kid. We came up here on a school trip,' Maja answered him, thinking about the fairy-tale town she'd passed through earlier. Ålesund, a picturesque, art deco town captured the essence of Norway. The buildings' facades ranged from pastel shades to vibrant jewel colours and perfectly complemented the deep green of the valleys, the Prussian blue fjords and the snow-capped mountains.

It was so very beautiful, a beauty that slapped you in the face and grabbed you by the heart.

And Ålesund, with the majestic Sunnmøre in the background and the dazzling waters of the fjords slapping the shore, was the prettiest stone in nature's jewellery box. 'I'll never forget the view from Aksla mountain,' Maja mused. 'Have you been?'

'I have,' Jens replied.

Maja half turned to face him. 'Sea, islands, mountains, all stretching as far as the eye can see. The day I went, it was glorious, a sunny clear day and I swear we could see for ever.'

Jens half smiled and her stomach flipped over. He was dressed in dark jeans, expensive trainers and a black loose, linen jacket over a white T-shirt. He looked fantastic, as a hot billionaire on holiday should.

With him her emotions were on a constant, unending roller-coaster ride, veering from resentment to attraction, dislike to desire. It was exhausting. Maja stared straight ahead, not wanting him to see the tumult in her eyes.

Feeling movement behind her, she watched the server place the cream-topped, whisky-flavoured coffee in front of her and thanked him. She lifted the glass and took a healthy sip, enjoying the rich combination of flavours and the hit of alcohol.

She looked over at Jens and saw his wince. 'Are you going to tell me that it's no way to drink good whisky?' she asked, lifting her eyebrows.

The smallest of smiles tugged the corners of his mouth. 'Would you listen to me if I did?' he asked.

Was he teasing her? Her answer would be the same either way. 'Of course not.'

Jens didn't intimidate her. He annoyed, frustrated and made her furious, but she wasn't intimidated.

His mouth definitely twitched. After finishing the last inch of his beer, he rested his big hands against his flat stomach. 'So, where are you staying tonight?'

Maja released a little sigh of pure pleasure. 'The hotel

manager has arranged for me to spend the night in the honeymoon suite. Hilda is staying in Ålesund.' Maja took another sip of her Irish coffee and looked at him over the rim of her glass. 'And you?'

His smile was slow, amused and sensual. 'Where else would I, as your fiancé, stay but with you, Maja?'

Cool and competent, Jens steered the SUV, a courtesy car loaned to him by the hotel's manager, towards Ålesund's harbour. Maja was quite certain he could ask for the moon, and it would be hauled down from the heavens. When you were a wildly rich man prepared to drop many millions on a wedding at the resort, what you asked for, you got.

She wished she could've refused his offer of a dinner cruise up the Geirangerfjord. She'd only agreed because her other option was to join him for dinner at the wonderfully romantic, stunningly intimate restaurant at Hotel Daniel-Jean. The cruise was the lesser of two romantic evils.

She was looking forward to the hustle of being on a busy, touristy boat. There was nothing romantic about being surrounded by camera-clicking people and it was exactly what she needed.

Maja sighed. The hotel was a dream destination for any bride, elegant and romantic. The exquisite ballroom could accommodate many guests, the extensive gardens were luxurious and incredible, and the wine list and food choices top drawer. The honeymoon suite was...*spectacular*.

How could she spend the night there with Jens? It was sublime, with an outside bath overlooking the fjord, a private deck, a massive bed to roll around in, Dom Perignon in ice buckets and expensive chocolates on pillows. Massive arrangements of white roses in silver vases scented the air. The suite screamed romance and great sex…

And she had to keep away from it for as long as possible because, in that romantic room, she might give into temptation and ask Jens to take her to bed.

If she did that, she'd be taking stupidity to new heights. He was blackmailing her, manipulating her into doing what he wanted. He intended to marry her, but she still didn't know why. Oh, he said he wanted revenge, but how would their marrying satisfy his need for payback? No, he had something else up his sleeve and until she knew what that was, she couldn't let her guard down.

And that meant no intimate dinners and only going back to the room when they had to…

Jens turned the SUV into a parking space and walked around the bonnet to open Maja's door. She sucked in crisp, clear, glacier-fresh air. The harbour was as busy as she expected it to be in the height of summer, with two sightseeing boats docked at the pier. Maja watched as people hurried up the gangplank, chattering excitedly.

Excellent. There were lots and lots, and lots, of people to dilute any wisps of romance.

Jens lifted her precious camera bag from the passenger-seat floor. 'Are you happy for me to carry it?'

She held out her hand to take it and Jens handed it over. The weight of the bag felt familiar and reassuring. When she met Jens's eyes she shrugged. 'My camera bag is like my security blanket,' she told him. 'When I'm not carrying it, I feel naked.'

'I get it,' Jens replied. He placed a hand on her back and guided her to the harbour. 'What do you want to do first? Go cruising or take a walk through Ålesund?'

Maja looked at the sightseeing boats. Judging by the excited tourists standing at the railings, and the almost empty gangway, the boats looked ready to leave. They would be the last on board, there was no time for a walk. But Jens didn't pick up his pace and didn't seem to be in any hurry to embark. Her dad had been the same...people, planes, trains, cars and ships departed on his schedule. Was it a billionaire thing?

The gangplanks on both ships started to rise, and Maja darted an anxious look at Jens. 'Jens, we'd better hurry up.'

'Why?' he asked, puzzled. 'And you didn't answer my question—do you want to take a look around Ålesund, or do you want to get on the water?'

Maja pointed to the sightseeing boats. 'I want to get on the water, but our boat is about to leave.'

Jens looked confused. 'That's not our transport. I couldn't think of anything worse than being cooped up with hundreds of people on a packed tourist ship, even for a few hours.'

It wouldn't be her first choice either, but she needed to be on a big boat to put some space and distance between her and Jens. Maja noticed a smaller boat in the inner harbour; it looked as if it would take about fifty guests. Not as many people, but it would do. Maybe that was their boat.

Jens placed a hand on her shoulder and steered her in that direction. They passed a few catamarans, a restored trawler and Jens slowed down when they approached an exquisite superyacht moored next to the smaller cruise vessel. Maja's heart kicked up at its sleek lines. It looked brand new. If it wasn't, then it hadn't been in operation for long.

'Forty-three metres long, five staterooms, hot tub, jet skis and a crew of seven,' Jens told her. 'Shall I tell you about the engine capacity and specifications?'

Back then, he'd enjoyed her love of the sea but had been confounded by her uninterest in the mechanics of the vessels that sailed it.

'I'm good,' Maja told him. Sure, the yacht was lovely, but they needed to get onto the boat moored next door. Like the others, it was ready to depart, and they needed to hurry up. The guests already on board stood at the railing or were claiming seats on the deck, settling in.

Maja started to walk towards the small ship. Jens's hand tugging her shirt stopped her fast walk to the boat. 'Where are you going?' he asked, lifting his eyebrows.

She gestured to the ship. 'I thought we were going on a fjord cruise, but if you don't hurry up, we're going to miss it.'

Jens jerked his thumb at the superyacht. 'We are, but on the *Daydreamer*. We'll be the only guests on board, so we'll get to decide where we are going, and for how long.'

A yacht? All to themselves? She sent a longing look to the vessel next door as her heart dropped to her toes. 'Oh.'

If they were lovers, and happy about being together, it would be wonderful to walk onto the sleek yacht hand in hand, looking forward to each other's company and to being alone as they took in the stunning scenery all around them.

But they weren't. Jens held her career in his hands, and she couldn't, mustn't forget that they were sliding into a marriage neither of them wanted all because Jens couldn't forgive and forget.

You could stop it, right now. If you just admitted that Maja Hagen is M J Slater, this would all go away. The reviews are in, you've established your credentials, and you have a major exhibition under your belt. Nobody could accuse you of trading on your father's famous name.

Maja bit the inside of her lip. She couldn't. Not yet. Maybe not ever. It was the one thing untainted or touched by a past that haunted her. She wasn't ready to give that up.

Maja held the strap of her camera bag, her fingers itching to capture the sleek lines of the boat, the white paintwork a dazzling contrast to the cerulean-blue sea.

'It looks amazing, Jens,' she reluctantly admitted.

'You haven't been on board yet,' he replied, sounding amused.

'No, but I did a photo shoot on a similar yacht a few years back and I know what to expect. Thank you for hiring her—'

A strange look crossed his face and Maja frowned. Wait…

'You did *hire* her, right?'

Jens tried to guide her to the yacht, but she planted her feet and waited for him to turn his attention back to her. 'Jens…what did you do?' she asked, lifting her eyebrows. She thought she knew but she wanted him to say it.

He scratched the side of his neck. 'My assistant couldn't find a private charter at such late notice and I'm not in the mood to be pleasant to strangers, so...' His words trailed off.

'You *bought* it?'

His powerful shoulders rose and fell. 'It's berthed here but the owner rarely used it. But she doesn't like to hire it out. I asked, she said no. So I offered to buy it and she said yes.'

Maja lifted her boot and ran it down the back of her calf as she took in his words. He made it sound so simple, but this yacht had to be worth more than ten million pounds, and he'd started negotiations no more than an hour ago. The man didn't let the grass grow under his feet...

Or whatever the seafaring equivalent of that saying was.

He sent a quizzical look at the boat. 'So, I now own a yacht.' He looked a bit puzzled at the thought and Maja's heart tumbled around her chest.

He placed a hand on her arm and squeezed. 'And she's a beauty. Shall we go and see what I bought, Maja?'

The *Daydreamer* was as luxurious as Maja expected but a great deal more spacious. The living-room area was impressive, panelled in expensive wood and dotted with cream-coloured seating, looking like a lounge out of a glamorous show house. The yacht also boasted a smaller den with a large screen to watch movies and a spectacular kitchen with all the mod cons. She followed the yacht's captain down to the master cabin and sighed at the huge king-sized bed covered with sparkling white linen. The en suite bathroom held his-and-hers sinks, a bath, a power shower and a separate toilet.

She very much approved. How could she not?

Jens and the captain left to explore the engine room and she looked around, thoroughly impressed. There was a hot tub on board, but she hadn't brought a swimming costume with her. Maybe she could quickly pop into Ålesund and buy one; she wanted to sit in the warm bubbles of the hot tub while drinking a glass of wine and watching the light bounce off the mountains and the fjord.

She wanted to sit in it with Jens, to admire his broad chest, what she knew was a ridged stomach, and his wide, muscled shoulders. Spirals of heat warmed her belly. Why was she still so attracted to him? Maja pulled open the nearest cupboard door and blinked at the array of dresses hanging in the space, tags still attached. These had to belong to the previous owner, left here so she didn't need to worry about packing. Her father had been the same— he'd kept duplicate items of clothing at his Olso and Bergen apartments, at their house in Svolvær, and in storage at various hotels around the world. Maja rolled her eyes. It wasn't hard to pack a bag or to get your staff to pack one for you.

Curious, she opened another cupboard and saw a couple of shirts. There were also dresses, capri pants, stylish, colourful clothing and all with their tags intact. Maja squinted at a tag, and noticed the clothes were designer and that they'd yet to be worn. Pulling open a drawer, she saw a pile of panties and bras, in various shades of the rainbow and styles. In another drawer, she found swimming costumes, including a black and white one-piece with high-cut legs and brightly patterned bikinis. She winced at the price. Wow. How could something with so little fabric cost so much?

She heard footsteps on the steps. Jens stopped halfway down the stairs, looked at the scarlet bikini in her hand, and raised one eyebrow. 'I approve. It's a great colour.'

'It's not mine. The wardrobe is stocked with clothes.' Maja placed the bikini back in the cupboard drawer and closed the door. 'So, are you happy with your purchase?'

'I am. I'm going to come back at some point and do a proper inspection.'

He was the CEO of a multibillion-dollar empire, and she knew time was a commodity in short supply. 'Do you still have your captain's licence?'

Maja wasn't surprised when he nodded. The sea was in his blood.

Jens walked down the last few steps and stepped into the cabin, a map in his hand. He looked around and nodded his approval. 'This is a nice master suite. Much bigger than the other four cabins.'

Before leaving the hotel he'd changed into cotton shorts and a loose, light blue button-down shirt. Her gaze slid over and down him, taking in the tanned v between the lapels of his shirt, the hint of the fine chest chair she'd loved to rub her nose in, and the bulge under the zip of his trousers. He wore no shoes. Like her, he'd kicked them off when they stepped onto the yacht, and Maja reacquainted herself with his very nice feet. Big, sure, but still elegant.

She could easily imagine him walking into the bedroom from the bathroom, with just a towel around his lean hips. The towel falling and him looming over her as she lay naked in bed, watching him with hungry eyes. Rolling over to straddle him, the early morning light streaming in from the windows, watching the stars out of that same window as she lay on his chest after making love…

He belonged in this room, with her. The thought rolled over her and she had to drop her eyes from his face, scared he'd read her mind. She was afraid he'd do something about relieving the sexual tension building between them, and even more scared he wouldn't.

But she couldn't keep her eyes off him for more than a minute and she saw his Adam's apple bob, and he rubbed the back of his neck. Yeah, he was also thinking about the best way to put this big bed to use.

One of them had to be sensible. They shouldn't rock the boat. Because if they started stripping off and sending clothes flying, they might never come up for air.

'What have you got there?' Maja asked, nodding at the map in his hand, happy her voice sounded normal.

He looked down, and it took him a few seconds to respond. She liked that she could throw this supposedly cool, always thinking, unemotional man off balance. Maybe if she kept doing that she'd be able to find the boy she'd loved beneath the layers Jens had built up over the last decade.

There was always the risk of him doing the same thing to her. Could she allow him to peek under the cover, past the barriers of protection she'd constructed? She didn't know how far they'd get, because the elephant in the corner— Jens blackmailing her into marriage—was always present.

Time would tell.

Jens spread the map on the bed and Maja walked over to him and looked down at the topographic map. Jens jabbed a spot with his short-nailed finger. 'We're here,' he said.

'I can think of worse places to be,' Maja assured him. 'So, what's the plan?'

'Well, food first, I'm starving.'

So was she. She'd snagged a chocolate-covered strawberry from a bowl in the honeymoon suite at the Hotel Daniel-Jean, but she'd eaten nothing substantial since leaving Bergen.

'I asked the chef to prepare a meal. Scallops for a starter, lobster for the main course, and sorbet, I can't remember the flavour, for dessert.'

He didn't ask her if she was happy with his selection, but he didn't need to. It was his boat, his staff and he could order what he wanted for dinner.

Honestly, she would've been satisfied with bangers and mash, but freshly caught seafood sounded amazing. Was it a coincidence that he'd remembered that scallops and lobster were her two favourite foods?

'That sounds perfect,' she told him.

They were in a stunning cabin, on an amazing yacht and were about to take a cruise, the only two people on board. She'd been worried about the romance of the hotel, and the honeymoon suite, but being alone on a luxurious yacht upped the sexy factor by a thousand per cent.

Oh, she was in a heap of trouble here. But, to be fair, she hadn't anticipated Jens buying a yacht! Who did that? Billionaires, apparently.

'So what would you like to do?' Jens asked. He looked down at the map, moved closer to her and Maja found her shoulder pressing into the top of his biceps. She didn't pull away and neither did he. Not smart…oh, well. 'We can either hug the coast, or I can ask the captain to head into Geirangerfjord and we can look at the Seven Sisters waterfall cascading down the cliffs.'

'That sounds good.'

He traced a route on the map. 'I wish we could carry on, head on up to Trondheim, Rorvik, and then into the Arctic Circle, Bodo and east to the Lofoten chain of islands.'

She did too. But that wasn't a trip they could take when there was so much distrust and residual damage between them. That was a trip for lovers, not for two people engaged in a battle of wills and emotional warfare, struggling to keep their hands off each other.

But this moment felt like a rare truce and she didn't want to go back to sniping at each other, not just yet.

She waved at the map. 'If you had a choice to go further, stay on this boat longer, where else would you go?' she asked him, aware she was leaning into him as she used to do. She didn't move away when his arm crossed her back and his hand loosely held her hip. They shouldn't touch like this, it was dangerous, but she wasn't going to make a big deal about it. Besides, she liked his hands on her. She always had.

'Svolvær,' he answered her, and her breath hitched. Svolvær was where they'd met and fallen in love. 'Well, east of Svolvær. I own a small island. I inherited it from my aunt.'

She'd love to go back to Svolvær, the place where it all started, the beginning of their story. She wondered if Håkon had still owned the Hagen holiday home in the small city when he'd died. The house she'd sneaked Jens into, the place where he'd initiated her into the wonderful world of sex. Well, it had started there…her education had continued on his boat and in his tiny apartment.

Hot now, Maja stepped away from him, jamming her hands into the back pockets of her pants to keep from reaching for him. She cleared her throat. 'Maybe you should tell the captain we're ready to leave,' she told him, her voice sounding a little ragged.

'That's a really good idea. We should go up.'

They should. Immediately. But neither of them moved. Jens watched her for a few seconds, his blue eyes pinning her to the spot. Maja held her breath as he lifted his hands and rested his thumbs on either side of her chin and he gently, so gently swept them up her jaw, pinpricks of delight following in their wake. He looked, just for a moment, a little disbelieving, as if he couldn't understand why she was here, how he came to be touching her. One thumb skated over her bottom lip while his other hand cradled her face, causing havoc to course through her body.

Don't kiss him…don't kiss him…don't…

Her feet rose to her toes, and her mouth aimed for his, and when their lips connected, Maja felt Jens tense. Would he turn away, would he kiss her back? Was this the worst idea in the world?

They hovered there, not moving, for just a second, and Maja felt Jens shudder and his hands, still holding her face, tightened, just a fraction. His sigh hit her lips and she waited to see what he would do. And then she waited some more, suspended. After what seemed like a minute, a month, a year, Jens's lips softened and he fed her a simple, sweet kiss and gently pulled away.

'We should go up,' Jens said, his words jagged, 'before we do something we regret.'

She should back down, step away, but she couldn't, not just yet. Maja fought the urge to apologise, to explain, to tell him she'd missed him, that he was always at the back of her mind, and that nobody affected her as he did.

Nobody raised her heartbeat and caused a firestorm in her belly, between her legs, nobody infuriated her and confused her as he did, nobody came close. He was an anomaly, a one-off, a constant source of confusion and the well of her want.

He walked into any room she was in, and the air disappeared, and the walls retracted, and her only thoughts were how long it would be before she found herself in his arms. How could she want, hate and crave him?

And why was she on this boat? Why had she put herself back in this position of wanting what she shouldn't, pretending that he hadn't upended her life, praying that she'd find the good, decent man she loved so much under the steel-hard revenge-seeker?

He doesn't want to hear your explanations, remember? He told you so.

Maja dropped back down to her feet and stepped back from his hold on her. She pushed her hair back and tried, and failed, to smile. 'Great. I could murder a glass of wine,' she said, trying to be brisk.

She walked away from him, heading for the stairs leading to the lounge area of the boat. From there she could walk out onto the deck and up to the top deck of the yacht. Maybe up there she'd find enough air to fill her lungs and get her brain working again.

And maybe it was time to accept that she was weak for him, that he was impossible to resist and that she and Jens would soon find themselves naked, together. And sooner rather than later.

CHAPTER SEVEN

THEY ANCHORED IN a secluded cove and, after a spectacular dinner of lobster and scallops on wild greens, followed by a light peach sorbet mousse, Jens refilled his and Maja's wine glasses from the bottle resting in the cooler. Then he sat next to her on the huge lounger on the wooden aft deck. He adjusted the cushions behind his back and sighed his appreciation. The deck ended two feet from the edge of the built-in lounger. The rest of the yacht was behind them, and in front of him was the fjord edged by steep cliffs. It was just past eleven at night and the falling sun was occupying itself by painting pink and purple streaks on the sky. It was absurdly quiet, and soul-stealingly beautiful.

Jens felt his shoulders drop and the cords in his neck relax, his stomach muscles loosen. He never realised how stressed or tense he was until he was out on the water. Only in these moments of quiet contemplation did he realise that his fourteen-to-sixteen-hour workdays, the endless meetings, being responsible for a workforce of more than fifteen thousand, took a mental and physical toll on him.

He always said he should take more time and visit his *hytte*—his wooden cabin on his island east of Svolvær—more often. He loved the outdoors, as most Norwegians did, but *friluftsliv*—the outdoors lifestyle Norwegians lived for—wasn't a priority.

He had to get back to it, to hike, to fish, to breathe fresh air and marvel at nature. He should schedule time to sit on the water drinking wine with a pretty girl.

He glanced at Maja's profile, taking in her glazed-over eyes, her slightly open mouth. She'd forgotten about the wine, him, and where they were. The artist in her was assimilating the colours, trying to work out how to recreate them, either on a canvas or on her computer using a complicated filter.

'Where's your camera?' he asked, surprised it wasn't in her hands.

'Right here.' She used her wine glass to gesture at the space next to her.

'You don't want to capture the sunset?'

She tipped her head, considering his question. He'd expected an immediate 'yes' and was surprised when she shook her head. 'Not this time.'

'Why wouldn't you want to?' he asked, curious.

She didn't pull her eyes off the sky. 'Because, later, the colours won't match up to my memory and I'll be disappointed. Sometimes we can't capture perfection and we dilute it if we do.'

Jens lifted his wine glass to his mouth, enjoying the slide of the cool liquid over his tongue. She was a mixture of philosophy and practicality, thoughtfulness, and pride. Sensitivity and seriousness. She was more than she was before, a deeper version of the girl he knew. And he wanted her with a need that bordered on insanity.

He still didn't know how he'd managed to stop himself

from lowering her to the bed earlier, how he'd resisted. It was his greatest act of self-restraint, bar none. He'd wanted nothing more than to undo the buttons of her shirt, push her trousers down her legs, and help her with her shoes. Slide her bra strap down her shoulder, feasting on every inch of skin revealed to him.

He'd managed to stop himself from stepping over the line, but he didn't know how much longer he could resist her. He knew he should. Making love to her was never part of the plan and would complicate the situation far more than was necessary.

This was the woman—fascinating or not, gorgeous or not that he was blackmailing into marrying him, the woman he was going to leave at the altar. If he slept with her, he'd be opening himself—them—up to piling sexual attraction upon long-ago hurts. It would be the equivalent of the *Daydreamer* ploughing into an iceberg.

He was staging this wedding to exact revenge, on her, her father, and to put his past behind him.

He heard the camera shutter whirr and looked right and into the lens of her camera. Why was she taking a photograph of him? He lifted his eyebrow. 'Really?'

A mischievous smile appeared on her lips, one he remembered her wearing a lot more often when they were younger. 'It would be a great stock photo, maybe its title could be "a billionaire on his boat".'

He smiled, reluctantly amused. 'You might earn enough royalties off it to buy a soda.'

'You're selling yourself short. I'd earn enough to buy a meal,' she teased. He'd missed this, missed Maja's sly and subtle humour. Twelve years ago, she'd tempered his ambition, reminded him to smell the roses, to slow down, relax. If they were together, properly, in a real relationship, he could easily imagine her mocking his wealth, reminding him not to take life so seriously, to slow down and enjoy the fruits of his hard work.

If she hadn't left…if Håkon…

Just give it a rest, Nilsen.

It was late, the sun was finally dipping behind the mountains, bringing an end to the long summer's day. The purple in the sky was now violet and the pinks were fading fast. It wasn't the time to discuss the past…there was nothing to *discuss.*

Jens downed the rest of his wine and put his glass on the deck next to him. He bent his knees and rested his wrists on them. He looked relaxed but he wasn't. As he knew Maja was, he was conscious of the sexual tension buzzing between them, the need and the want. Like him, she was fighting temptation. He didn't know if she was winning or losing, all he knew was that it was getting harder, by the second, to sit here and not touch her.

Maja placed her camera back in her bag, snapped it closed and placed it on the table behind her. When she looked back at him, her eyes locked on his. Would she make the first move? Would he? Who would cave first? Because someone would…

Jens rolled off the lounger and stood up, walking to the railing and gripping it, his knuckles immediately turning white.

If you sleep with her, you can't jilt her. You can't make love to her and then leave her at the altar. That isn't fair…

None of this was fair. It wasn't fair that his mum had

abandoned him, that Maja had dumped him, Håkon had tried to ruin him. Life wasn't fair, he knew and lived that truth. He'd done some things he wasn't proud of, made some tough business calls that might've been legal but not, necessarily, honourable and he always regretted them after the deal was done. If he slept with Maja, knowing he intended to jilt her, he'd feel the same way.

He was a cold, unemotional bastard and blackmailing her into marriage was bad enough. But sleeping with her knowing that he would leave her at the altar later was a line he didn't think he could cross.

Jens didn't look back at her when he spoke. 'I'll tell the captain to take us back to port.'

Maja didn't answer him and when he turned around to look at her, he caught the soft smile on her face. 'Why don't we stay on the boat tonight, and take the day tomorrow, maybe even stay tomorrow night too? It's lovely out here, and so quiet. I think you need some quiet, Jens. I know I do.'

He did. He hesitated, weighing up the pros and cons. Con: being alone with her was a temptation, he didn't know if he could resist her. Pros: the serenity and, as she said, the quiet.

Then Maja wrinkled her nose. 'But the hotel manager did give me the honeymoon suite for free. I feel bad for not taking him up on his offer.'

If he could buy a bloody yacht, he could pay for a hotel suite they didn't use. He looked around and knew he wasn't ready to return to Ålesund. 'I'll make it worth his while,' he told her. 'And if we tell him we'll have the wedding there, he'll be more than happy.'

Maja stiffened and Jens winced. The talk of their marriage always managed to kill the mood. He sighed. 'Shall we stay on the water, or shall we go back in, Maja?'

She hesitated, but when she looked at their amazing surroundings, he knew her answer. 'Stay.'

He swallowed his sigh of relief. 'You can have the cabin we looked at earlier, help yourself to clothes,' he briskly told her. He wasn't going to make love to her. *He couldn't.* He'd reined in his imagination and was thinking clearly again. But in case he slipped again, he thought it better to put his cards on the table so there couldn't be any misconceptions or misunderstandings.

'No matter what happens between us, Maja, we're still getting married.' And he'd still jilt her. He gestured to the boat, then the view. 'This is lovely, but it changes nothing.'

'Message received.' Maja nodded, her expression unreadable. Instead of speaking, she lifted her wine glass. 'Could you get me some more wine? I plan on spending a few more hours here, inhaling the view and enjoying the quiet. Would you like to be quiet with me, Jens?'

He could do that. Just for a few hours.

Jens hadn't expected to get much sleep—he never did— so he was surprised he slept a solid six hours on the wide lounger on the aft deck, covered by a light blanket. After a breakfast of *vafler*, Norwegian waffles topped with cloudberries, he needed to exercise, and was desperate to stretch his muscles. He told the deckhand, Lars, to unload the yacht's jet skis while he swam to the shore and back, an easy mile.

When he returned, Lars was attempting to teach a bemused Maja how to ride the jet ski. She looked completely befuddled by the powerful machine and Jens left Lars to it. The younger man had more patience than he did, so he climbed onto the most powerful of the two machines and took off, loving the wind in his hair and the power between his legs. He skimmed across the water, indulging his inner speed freak. After an hour of doing tricks and turns, hauling out some old skills, his body felt loose and his muscles warm, and he headed back to the *Daydreamer*. He stopped a fair way from the yacht and turned his back to the handlebars to watch Maja on the jet ski. She was barely going faster than he could swim, but she looked as though she was having fun.

Her curls were tighter, damp from sea spray, and her life jacket didn't quite manage to hide her curves. She wore the scarlet bikini she'd found in the cabin, and he thoroughly approved.

Jens yawned and tipped his head up to the sun. When last did he take a day off? Ages ago. He'd last been on a jet ski ten years back. He grinned as Maja let out a screech as she took a turn too fast, smiling at her huge grin of delight when she managed to steady the jet ski without flipping it over.

It was nice to sit here, not thinking about his business, about the wedding. Oh, both hovered on the edges of his mind, but he refused to give them space. He was allowed, wasn't he, to take a day off from the pressures of both?

Aunt Jane wouldn't approve, she always felt deeply uncomfortable doing nothing. He smiled at the memory of his irascible aunt, seventeen years older than his mum, forced to take him on when she'd chosen to remain a spinster and childless. She'd been forthright and unaffectionate, but she'd loved him in her own way. As much as she could.

He'd felt safe with her. And that was the biggest compliment he could pay anyone. She was still the only person who always did what she said and who'd never let him down. He couldn't imagine her on this vessel, in his house in Bergen. She'd be bemused by his wealth, definitely unimpressed.

Jens flipped his sunglasses onto his face as he watched Maja chugging over to him, the jet ski idling just enough to keep her moving forward. Man, she drove like a granny, and it made him smile.

She slowly braked and eventually, about three years later, drifted over to him, her eyes sparkling as she faced him.

'That was so much fun! Exhilarating!'

He grinned at her and folded his arms to keep from curling his hand around her neck and pulling her in for a kiss. 'You didn't go fast enough to hit exhilarating. I doubt you went faster than a geriatric on sleeping tablets.'

She wrinkled her nose at him, and he grinned, feeling light-hearted and relaxed. If he pulled her onto his jet ski and draped her legs over his, they could make love right here, right now. The thought hit him out of nowhere.

You're not going to make love to Maja, remember? That would complicate everything.

His brain got it, but the rest of his body wasn't interested in being sensible.

'I was being cautious,' Maja responded, pulling him back to reality. 'It's my first time on a jet ski. I didn't want to fall off!'

Because he liked the spark in her green and gold eyes,

he flickcd the toggle of her life jacket. 'That's what life jackets are for.'

'The water, in case you didn't notice, is freezing! Not all of us have ice in our veins, Nilsen!'

Jens frowned. Was that what she thought? That he had ice in his veins? He considered her words and reluctantly admitted she wasn't far off the mark. For more than a decade, he'd operated in a state of suspended animation, not allowing his blood to heat, finding little amusement in anyone or anything.

IIe was ruthless, cold and hard, but he got the job done.

Maja laid a hand on his forearms and squeezcd. IIer eyes, when hc looked into them, flashed with remorse. 'That came out wrong, Jens, I didn't mean to criticise you. I was only referring to your insane tendency to swim in cold water.'

She looked sincere and that might be true, but therc was no escaping the reality of who he was. Circumstances and choices, his and others, had forced him to eschew emotion and shut down. It worked for him, he'd built a mammoth business and had power and influence.

But Maja dropping back into his life had him second-guessing himself.

It was a beautiful morning. The hot sun bounced off the blue water and a white-tailed eagle flew in lazy circles high above his head. This was a very rare day off and he didn't want to spoil it by arguing with Maja. He simply wanted to be a guy on a jet ski in the company of a pretty woman, taking in the outstanding scenery. Their issues could wait and, for as long as he was on the yacht, he would shove all thoughts of revenge to the back of his mind. He was allowed to step away for a few hours, maybe even a day, wasn't he?

Before he could talk himself out of his decision, he lifted his finger to his lips and released a piercing whistle. The deckhand immediately responded by walking to the railing.

'Sir?' he called.

'Maja and I are going for a spin up the coast. Do you feel like a swim, Lars? If not, we'll pootle over to you,' he said. 'We might get there next year but we'll get there.'

'It'll be quicker if I swim over,' Lars replied, grinning.

'Oh, ha-ha!' Maja muttered, rolling her eyes.

Lars whipped off his shirt, dived into the water and Jens noticed Maja's shudder. The kid was a fish, he noticed, impressed by his strong stroke. As Lars swam over to them, Jens helped Maja onto his jet ski, telling his lower body to behave when her thighs gripped the outside of his thighs. Her arms encircled his waist, and she rested her chin on his shoulder. 'Not too fast, Jens,' she warned him.

That would be a problem as he had only two speeds: fast and very fast.

'I won't flip this beast over,' he told her as Lars reached her jet ski and hauled himself up. Jens gunned the accelerator and pulled away. Maja chose that exact moment to let go of her grip on his waist, and she flew off the jet ski and plopped into the water.

She bobbed on the surface, her hair hanging in rats' tails down her face. He slowed down as he did a wide turn and puttered over to her, cutting the engine when he came close. Maja glared at him and launched an impressive stream of water at his face. 'You said I wouldn't fall off!'

In fairness, he'd said he wouldn't flip the jet ski, not that she wouldn't fall off. But Jens, because he was too smart to say that to a blue-lipped Maja, reached down, grabbed her by the wrist and easily hauled her onto the jet ski. 'I suppose you want to go back and jump into a warm shower?' he asked, disappointed in advance. The sun was hot, and she'd dry off in no time, but he knew Maja wasn't a fan of being cold.

Instead of agreeing with him, she manoeuvred her leg over the side of the jet ski, snuggled in behind him and wrapped her arms around her waist, her grip anaconda tight. 'Now you can go. I'd tell you to go slow but that's not in your nature but, word of warning, if I go off again, you're coming too.'

He grinned. Was he having fun? Maybe. It had been so long he'd forgotten what that felt like.

Maja swirled the cognac around in her balloon glass, burying her nose in the glass and inhaling its base notes of maple, molasses and nuts. After another spectacular dinner, perfectly cooked Wagyu steaks and *frites*, Jens dismissed his staff, and they made their way to the aft deck to enjoy the royal-blue and bright pink sunset. Maja sank down onto the wide cushions, stretching out her legs. She was happy, tired and very relaxed. By silent agreement, she and Jens ignored their upcoming wedding, their shared past, and any other contentious subjects. They'd laughed a little, smiled a lot, simply enjoying the stunning day, the six-star service by the yacht crew and the amazing scenery.

Tomorrow they'd be hurtled back into the reality of their situation. But would Jens allow them to have tonight? She hoped so. Something about being on this yacht and away from her real life, Bergen and their situation made her feel brave. Or maybe she would be voicing what they both wanted. She knew he desired her as much as she did him. The heat between them wasn't going anywhere. Maybe if they got it out of their systems, they could move past it. They could set each other on fire—just looking at each other made sparks fly and wildfires start. Despite the issues between them, and their complicated pasts, they'd been building up to this since they'd reunited weeks ago. How they'd lasted this long, Maja didn't know.

She watched as he sat next to her, relaxing on the reclining cushions, his long fingers wrapped around the bowl of his glass. With his messy hair and stubbled cheeks, and slightly sunburned nose, he looked younger tonight than he normally did, and not nearly as remote.

He looked like the young man she'd been so in love with.

'I want to make love with you.'

Maja was shocked that the words slipped out so easily, and nearly slapped her hand against her mouth.

Jens stared at her with burning eyes, but he didn't move a muscle and Maja knew that if she wanted him naked, she would have to make the move. She put her glass down and scooted closer to him and lowered her head to skim her lips across his mouth. How could something so wrong feel so very right?

Should she stop this now, while she could? Sensible Maja said yes, but she wasn't interested in anything *she* had to say. She wanted Jens, she craved him. She needed him, needed tonight. Maja knew she was playing with a firestorm and that it had the potential to consume her. But she didn't care. With him, it didn't matter she was dancing with fire. She was prepared for the lick of flame, the searing of her skin and her soul.

'This isn't a good idea, Maja.'

'I know, but so what?' She lifted her shoulders in a careless shrug. 'I'm so tired of doing what I should, Jens, what's sensible and safe. I want you to make love to me. I need you inside me, completing me, making me feel the way only you can.'

'How do I make you feel, Maja?' he asked, his thumb rubbing the length of her collarbone.

She lifted her hand to hold his face, her fingers skating over the short stubble on his jaw. 'You make me feel like me,' she replied. And it was true: naked in his arms, everything superfluous melted away and she became the essence of who she was, unimpeded by her birth name. She liked being Jens's lover, she always had.

She turned her head, found his lips with hers and knew this was where she wanted to be, right now, possibly for ever. His mouth covered hers and then his tongue was inside her mouth, seeking, taking, exploring. He made her feel as if she were surfing the edges of a tornado, flying over the edge of a snowy cliff, surfing a monster wave.

He tasted of the cognac they'd been drinking, tinged with the colours of the sunset they'd watched sink between the mountains and behind the sea. He tasted of deep purples, and violet indigos, of masculine intensity and raunchy sex. He tasted wild and free, and she wanted more.

She wanted everything he could give her.

Jens pulled his mouth off hers to look down at her and, in the romantic lighting in this area of the yacht, she saw the sexy combination of need and longing in his eyes.

He groaned. 'You're killing me, Maja.'

'You'll kill me if you don't take me inside and make love to me, Jensen,' Maja informed him, pushing her nose into his neck and inhaling the scent of sea and soap. She wouldn't ask again. Jens would either take her up on her offer or this was as far as they would go...

Maja waited for him to make up his mind, conscious of his fingers on her butt pushing into her flesh. She knew he was running scenarios, weighing up the pros and cons, but she thought that with every few passing seconds he lost a little tension, and became a little more relaxed.

Maybe, just maybe she'd get lucky. Maybe he'd kiss her neck again, run his lips over her jaw, down her neck, lick the top of her breast...

Maja was midway through her fantasy when he yanked her shirt up her body and cold air hit her skin. Her eyes slammed into his and within those dark depths she saw frustration—with himself or with her?—and pent-up desire. Despite it being chilly, she remained on her knees, her nipples pebbling against the lace of her bra. She swallowed when she saw Jens looking at her as though she was everything he'd been waiting for, all he'd ever wanted.

He cupped her breast, testing its weight, and his thumb rolled across her nipple, and pleasure skittered through her, into her womb and between her legs. He did it again, and she arched her back and released a small gasp.

'Do you like that?' he growled.

'You know I do,' Maja replied, her voice sexy and scratchy. 'Do it again.'

He teased her other nipple before lowering his head to pull it, fabric and all, into his mouth. The night air rattled over her body, but she didn't care. The appreciation she saw in his eyes and the need on his face created a warm buzz within her. Nothing mattered but Jens loving her...

Jens yanked her towards him, and her legs wrapped around his hips. He rose to his feet, easily holding her weight. After dragging his mouth across hers, he walked her into the lounge and steered left to walk down the narrow hallway leading to the master suite. The lounge and galley were deserted, and the running lights tossed shadows onto Jens's face.

He walked down the stairs, deposited her on the bed and leaned over her. He brushed her hair off her face and lightly gripped her chin. 'I didn't bring protection, did you?'

Maja had to think. No, she had a box in Edinburgh, but sex hadn't been on her mind when she'd packed for Norway. She shook her head. 'But I'm on one of those fancy IUDs,' she told him, forcing herself to think. 'And it's been a while so I'm clean.'

He nodded. 'I always use condoms, so I am too,' he told her. He ran his hand down her chest, creating a band of fire before stopping at the button of her jeans. 'Are you sure, Maja?'

She stroked her fingers through his hair. It was as soft as she remembered. 'Yes. I *need* you. I need this.'

Jens, with his hands on either side of her head, fed her a long kiss, and Maja locked her arms around his neck, welcoming his weight, his chest flattening her breasts. His tongue invaded her mouth and tangled with hers, pushing her for more, testing to see the depths of her passion.

Hers matched his, and Maja knew there was a good possibility of them setting this room on fire, possibly even the boat. She pushed her hand up and under Jens's shirt, needing her hands on his bare skin. His back was a series of dips and hollows, smooth skin over hard muscle.

Jens pulled back to grab a fistful of material behind his neck. He yanked the fabric and his shirt slid over his head. Instead of returning to the bed to kiss her, he stood up and Maja leaned back on her elbows, her eyes sweeping over his broad chest, taking in his toned abs and lean hips. A trail of dark hair snaked into his trousers and the moisture in her mouth disappeared when he pushed his trousers and underwear down. He was better than a fantasy, real and hot and *here*. Jens sent her a crooked smile.

'Like what you see?' he asked, his tone low and harsh.

She did. 'Very much so,' she assured him. 'I like the older version of you as much as I did the younger.'

He reached for the band of her trousers and his hot fingers slid between the material and the bare skin of her stomach and Maja gasped. So *good*. Impatient, she batted his hands away and flipped open the clasp and pushed her trousers down her hips, sighing when Jens pulled the fabric down her thighs with a sharp jerk. He took in her tiny panties and dragged his finger down her stomach and over her lace-covered mound. He pulled aside the fabric to look at her, his expression pure appreciation. 'You are so very beautiful, Maja, every inch of you.'

Jens dropped to his knees on the floor between her legs and Maja sucked in a deep breath. He couldn't be, no, he wasn't going to…but then he did, and his hot mouth was on her, seeking, probing, lifting her…higher, higher.

This was such an intimate expression of desire and Maja never allowed her other lovers the intimacy of this act.

Only Jens knew how to kiss her, to love her this way, and it was a memory of him she never wanted to be tainted. Maja pushed her fingers into his hair, her breath coming in short, rapid fits and starts. She loved this, loved the combination of his fingers and mouth, his slick tongue and clever lips, but, for their first time after so long, she wanted more.

She needed him inside her, filling all those places where he fitted best, rocking her up and over. She needed to hear his ragged breath and him calling her name as he came.

Sitting up, she gripped his shoulders and when he looked up at her, she stroked the tip of her finger over his forehead. 'I want you inside me, Jens. This first time after so long...'

He didn't need any further explanation, he simply rolled to his feet in a fluid motion and placed his hands on either side of her head, lowering his body to connect with hers. Maja's knees opened and he settled himself between her legs, hot and hard and masculine. He gripped her thigh and pulled it up and over his hip, as his erection probed her slick entrance. The sound of their breathing, hers rapid and his harsh, filled the cabin, and the air around them heated. Maja, bombarded with sensation, closed her eyes.

'No, look at me as I take you,' Jens commanded her, and her eyes flew open. He looked like the man he was, demanding and rugged, less smooth than he normally was. She liked him wild and untamed. A little unhinged. She loved that she could make him feel that way.

He balanced himself on one hand, his other still on her thigh as he slowly, too slowly, slid inside her. This...*him*... was what she needed, what she'd been missing. Jens pushed inside her and rocked his hips and a million torches ignited deep inside her, spreading heat and light into her. Maja lifted her hips, rocked against him and felt a ripple of tension course through him. He was barely holding on and she liked—loved!—that she could make this hard man burn for her.

Jens moved his hand from her hip under her butt and lifted her into him, and Maja tilted her hips, gasping when his shaft rubbed against a spot deep inside her, causing her to shudder. She rocketed up, unable to stop the tide of light and colour and sensation.

She shivered with anticipation and then she fell, tumbling and twisting in a maelstrom of light. She heard Jens calling her name, urging her on, but his words came from far away and she vaguely felt him tense, before releasing deep inside her.

As she floated down, Maja drifted her hand down his back, not able to breathe but deciding it didn't matter. She'd missed his weight on top of her, his strong body covering hers, his deep voice urging her to take more, telling her how much he craved her, how sexy she was.

He was the best lover she'd ever had, the only one she'd ever lost control with. The only one she wanted.

Making love, and giving each other pleasure, were something they truly excelled at, and when they conversed without words there were never any misunderstandings. But their mouths, their pride and their past got them into trouble.

But for now, in the warm cabin, listening to the slap of water against the hull, his body heavy on hers...this felt good. More frightening, it felt right. As if he was the only man who was supposed to be in her bed. And in her life.

This wasn't how she should feel about a man who was blackmailing him into marrying her.

CHAPTER EIGHT

THEY MADE IT back to the honeymoon suite at the Hotel Daniel-Jean late the next day, sleep deprived and buzzy from making love. They both needed rest and when Jens requested the room for another night, the hotel manager quickly agreed. After some heady kissing and heavy petting in the shower, they stumbled to the bed around six and instantly fell asleep, with Maja's head on Jens's shoulder, and half her body lying on his.

When she woke, Maja decided it was the best sleep she'd had in a decade. She was also ravenous. Maja gently lifted Jens's watch, saw that it was nearly eleven and considered closing her eyes again. She was about to when Jens rolled her onto her back and positioned himself between her thighs. After a long, deep kiss her thighs dropped open and Jens entered her, as slow and as soft as a lazy spring morning. He brushed her hair back from her face and watched her as he moved his hips, his fjord-blue eyes clocking her every gasp, sigh, and smile.

Once or twice he seemed to be on the verge of releasing an endearment or allowing soft words to fall onto her skin, but at the last moment, he hauled them back. But his body spoke to hers in sexy and sinful ways. Then Jens slid his hand between their bodies and found her hot button, causing her to shudder, then shake and she forgot everything else. She crested, and he followed moments later with a harsh groan.

After they cleaned up and pulled on the soft cotton robes the hotel provided, Maja walked onto the private balcony and sat down on the comfortable wooden bench swing, tucking her feet up under her bottom. Inside, she heard Jens talking to the waiter delivering their late supper and a bottle of wine.

Ten minutes later, Jens walked onto the deck and handed her a glass of wine and sat the bottle on the pretty wrought-iron table.

'There's a steak ceviche, lobster tails and a green salad inside. I also ordered *tilslørte bondepiker*.'

The dessert—whipped cream, apple sauce, and bread-crumbs roasted in sugar—was one of her favourite treats.

He sat down next to her and, using one foot, rocked the bench. After tucking a pillow behind his head, he released a satisfied sigh. She wondered if he'd bring up the subject of the wedding and this venue and was glad when he didn't. She wasn't ready to confront reality. She'd liked the bubble they'd been occupying the last thirty-six hours and didn't want it to be popped...not just yet.

On the table, Jens's phone buzzed, and he used voice activation to answer it. He pulled Maja's thigh over his and curled his hand around her knee. He spoke in Norwegian, and when she heard a gravelly voice return his greeting, she instantly recognised the voice of the captain of the *Daydreamer*.

'Captain Sig, I'm not sure if I'm going to do a proper inspection of the yacht in the morning,' Jens told him.

The captain spoke rapidly and because Maja's Norwegian was very rusty, she wasn't sure she understood everything they said. When Jens ended the call, she half turned to face him. 'What was that about a fishing boat?'

'A fishing trawler caught fire about fifty miles north of Svolvær. He told me because he knew I sailed out of the same harbour as the owner of the boat in distress.'

Maja knew how dangerous a fire on a sea vessel could be. 'Did the crew get off?' she asked, immediately worried.

Jens nodded. 'Thankfully. They were rescued by a trawler who heard their mayday call. No injuries, but the boat is leaking oil and is still on fire.'

'Do you know the owner of the boat? From…before?'

Jens closed his eyes and his fingers dug into her skin. 'Yes, it was owned by Gunnar Solberg.'

Solberg… Maja recognised the name. 'Didn't Gunnar Solberg work for you and your aunt?' Maja asked.

'Mmm. After you left, he borrowed money from your father, bought a couple of trawlers and went into competition with us. Gunnar poached some of our crew and tried to grab our quotas. But, like so many other small operators, Gunnar is barely holding on. The boat that's on fire is his only vessel, and his crew won't have work now.'

She felt sorry for Gunnar, but she was stuck on why her father had meddled in the Svolvær fishing scene after she left Norway. It was small fry to him, and it went against his selfish nature for him to loan money to a small-time fisherman. That wasn't his style. Unless there was something in it for him. She started to ask Jens what he knew, but he held up his hand and instructed his phone to call Captain Sig again.

Maja concentrated hard to understand their rapid conversation. 'Is a vessel en route to tow Gunnar's trawler into the nearest harbour?' Jens asked the captain.

'There is, but it's a few days away. Even with the insurance money, assuming Gunnar kept up with the payments, rumour has it that he won't be able to afford to tow the boat in, repair it and get back to sea.'

Jens told the captain to hang on, took a sip of his coffee and gripped the bridge of his nose and closed his eyes. He did that when he was thinking through a problem. After a minute, he lifted his head and tossed a series of commands into the phone.

When he cut the call, she raised her eyebrows. 'You're paying to have his boat towed and repaired? The salaries of his crew while they are out of work? Why? It doesn't sound like he was loyal to you.'

Jens shrugged. 'Most of his crew are older men, some of whom are close to retirement, and they'll struggle to find work if he doesn't provide it. Gunnar also has a sick wife and an autistic son. He doesn't need this hassle on top of everything else he has to deal with.'

Maja remembered how proud the fishermen were, how much they hated to be pitied. 'I'm surprised Gunnar would accept your help,' she mused. And she was shocked that he still had his finger on the pulse of Svolvær's fishing scene.

'He won't. That's why I'll run the expenses through the foundation I set up to help fishermen and their dependants. No one knows I run and fund it. Well, Sig does now, but I've asked him to keep my involvement quiet.'

Clever. Maja was impressed by his easy offer. And surprised. In so many ways he was exactly like her dad, then in others, the complete opposite. Håkon would never have stepped in to help a 'simple' fisherman repair his boat, or have it towed, especially if it cost him time or money. Jens didn't hesitate. He was such a conundrum…one Maja couldn't work out. He could be unbelievably harsh, a clone of her ruthless father. Then he did something kind and thoughtful, and she didn't know which side of him dominated. Apart from being the man who made her body sing, who was he?

Jens reached for the newspaper he'd placed on the table and flipped it open, his eyes running over the headlines. She placed her feet beneath her bottom, her eyes dancing over the unfamiliar letters. She'd let her Norwegian slide. There was only one picture on the front page, that of a dark-haired woman, and she instantly recognised the face of the famous musical theatre star.

'What's Flora been up to now?' she idly asked. 'A new show, another hit or an even younger lover?'

Jens stiffened and when his eyes met hers, she pulled back, blasted by the ice in them. 'I can't tell you how little I care about some egotistical Broadway star.'

Whoa! His voice was colder than his eyes. It had just been an offhand comment, and she couldn't understand his sharp reply. He tossed the newspaper onto the table and stood up and stomped into the bedroom. When he returned, he wore navy shorts and a white button-down shirt. And a remote expression on his face.

Maja reached for the newspaper and squinted down at the article, forcing her brain to translate the words. She got the gist: Flora was being nominated for an award, something about her being a credit to Norway. She turned her attention to Jens, who stood a few yards from her, his arms folded and his expression belligerent. What was it about this entertainer that set his teeth on edge?

'Do you know Flora? Have you met her?' she probed, needing to understand his reaction.

Jens snorted. 'You could say that.'

Right, he was back to being emotionally remote and inaccessible. *Fabulous*. But, because she was curious, she pushed for more. 'How do you know her, Jens?'

His smile was shark-like and held no humour. 'Oh, in the most biblical way of all.'

He'd *slept* with her? Right, that was more information than she needed.

Jens's eyes bored through her. 'I wasn't one of her many lovers, Maja.' He sighed. 'Although she would deny it with her dying breath, Flora is my mother.'

That was the last thing she'd expected to hear. And the pain bubbling under what was supposed to be a toss-away statement had her cocking her head, intrigued. Then again, everything about him fascinated her. 'Tell me more, Jens.'

Jens wasn't surprised by her question. He'd opened the door by mentioning his relationship to Flora and he'd silently invited Maja to indulge her curiosity about his past. Within the space of a day, they'd come to a point where she felt comfortable enough to pry into his life. Did she think they were on their way back to being friends and lovers?

They weren't. He couldn't let them be.

Jens walked back into the suite, carrying his wine glass.

He was already wrestling with how he was going to carry out his plans for revenge now that he'd made love to her. He'd known, dammit, that making love to her would complicate everything, but he'd been unable to resist her...

Still couldn't.

How would he get the outcome he wanted if he didn't follow through with this course of action? How would he get his revenge now? Every time he thought about their fake wedding and his plan to leave her at the altar, he felt fidgety. He didn't know if he could do it, whether he should.

Maybe if he told her about Flora, maybe if she realised how dysfunctional and messed up he was, she'd slam on brakes, and he wouldn't have to. It was a coward's way out, he knew that. But if she knew that his mother's casual cruelty and lack of interest caused him to be cold-hearted and hard-boiled, then she'd pull back and they'd be back on the same footing they were in Bergen. Maybe he'd be able to put some distance between them again. It was worth a shot. But he'd only give her the bare minimum, just enough information to make her understand he was irredeemable.

He took a seat at the wrought-iron table and tapped the newspaper with his index finger.

Stay cold, Nilsen. Unemotional. Inaccessible. Do not let her see how much your mother leaving affected you.

'Flora is the woman who birthed me. She's currently starring in a production in the West End. She'll be in Oslo next week to accept an award for her contribution to Norwegian art and culture.'

He forced himself to look at her and Maja's eyebrows, as he expected them to, flew up and shock jumped into her eyes.

'Can't you see the resemblance between us?' he asked. It was one of the reasons his mother gave him a wide berth if they happened to be at the same A-list function. Anyone seeing them together would immediately know they were related. They had the same eyes, the same nose and mouth.

'I can, actually,' Maja admitted, glancing at the paper. 'You look like a masculine version of her. She must've had you when she was very young.'

'She was eighteen when I was born, she's in her mid fifties now,' he answered, sounding as if he couldn't get enough air. He always got uptight when he thought about his mother. And since he'd never spoken about her to anyone, it was no wonder his heart wanted to jump out of his chest. He needed to take it down a notch. Or ten.

'She looks good.'

'Yeah, it's amazing what surgeons, a strict diet, plastic surgery and collagen injections can do.' Now he sounded bitter and resentful. Well, he *was* bitter and resentful.

'How did you come to live with Jane?' Maja asked.

Should he continue this conversation or cut it off? He had an internal debate and decided that as she was his fiancée— manoeuvred into the position or not—he could give her a little more information than most. 'We lived in Oslo,' he said, his words scalpel sharp. 'Flora was a dancer at a club.'

He didn't want to explain Flora had been an exotic daughter. 'Was it a…' she hesitated '…gentlemen's club?'

He nodded, just once. Maja, thankfully, didn't ask whether Flora provided services other than dancing. It was a question he'd never asked and didn't want to know the answer to.

'How did she go from working there to being a West End star?'

Jens drew patterns on the newspaper with his finger. 'One of the entertainers, a singer, didn't arrive for work one night and she filled in. Fortuitously, it was the very night a musical theatre producer from Broadway was in the room. He shipped her off to New York and she sent me to her sister.'

'And your dad?'

He was a blank space on his birth certificate. 'No idea.' He doubted Flora knew who his father was either.

Maja didn't react to his sharp statement. 'Why didn't your mum take you to London with her?'

Ah, the million-dollar question. The one he'd asked himself a million times as a kid. According to Jane, he couldn't go because Flora moved into a communal house-share. There wasn't space for him, and it wasn't a good 'environment'. Then, as her star rose, the excuses not to have him with her just got bigger and bolder. It was better for him to stay in Svolvær, to be raised as a Norwegian—between rehearsals and shows, she didn't have time to spend with him. But there was no way he'd let Maja hear him whine.

'Simply, she couldn't be bothered to be a mother.'

He felt uncomfortable with the sympathy he saw in her eyes and looked away. He didn't need it from her, or from anyone. Why had he opened this door, let her stroll on through?

'How often do you speak to her, see her?'

This was harder to answer, tougher to admit. 'I haven't seen my mother since she dropped me off with Aunt Jane a few days after my fifth birthday. For the first few years,

I received the odd phone call, a letter now and again. When I was eighteen—'

He stopped abruptly, not wanting to revisit that memory. He hated that, even after so long, he still wanted his mum to acknowledge him, introduce him to her world as her son. Why was that still so difficult for her to do? He was now successful, wildly so, rich, and educated. While he couldn't claim to be charming, he knew how to conduct himself in public.

Flora shouldn't be ashamed of him. Or maybe she was? Ashamed of the son who reminded her of the way she'd lived before achieving her own success.

Why was he dwelling on her? She wasn't worth his time or energy, and she shouldn't form part of his emotional landscape. He didn't need her. He didn't need *anyone*.

'What happened when you were eighteen, Jens?'

Nobody, not even Jane, knew about his abortive trip to London, how he stood outside the stage door for hours in the rain begging the security guard to let him see Flora.

Jens rolled his empty glass between the palms of his hands. 'Long story short, I stood outside her theatre for six hours one day, eight the next, trying to get to see her. I finally got a note to her through a security guard.' Jens had written three bullet points on that note: Jane, Svolvær and that he was either going to see her or he'd find a journalist interested in his story. 'She wasn't thrilled to see me.'

Maja let him talk, she didn't push him, and he appreciated that.

'When I got to her dressing room, she was in a temper. She demanded to know what I wanted, what the hell I was doing there.'

'You just wanted to see her, you were hoping to reconnect,' Maja stated as she lifted her feet onto the bench and wrapped her arms around her knees.

Exactly. 'She didn't want to.'

That was a mild description of their conversation. Flora had brutally told him she wasn't interested in him and never had been. He'd asked whether she'd ever admit he was her son, she'd made it clear she never would. He was an embarrassment and didn't fit into her world. Then she'd offered him money to go away and told him that whatever the papers offered him for his story, now or in the future, she'd double it to keep her from being associated with him.

'How did you leave things with her?' Maja asked, anger turning her eyes gold.

Jens gripped the bridge of his nose before answering her. 'She spoke, I listened, and then I walked out without saying another word.'

He sometimes wondered if Flora had ever done an Internet search on him, whether she ever saw the newspaper articles detailing his business successes. She had to know about his successful career—he'd been interviewed often and photographed on many red carpets and at celebrity events. But she never reached out and her silence was an ongoing reminder that she'd simply acted as an incubator for a child she'd never wanted. He was a long-ago stain on her youth, something to be ignored and dismissed.

He was in his mid-thirties and she'd yet to acknowledge him. If he was honest with himself, he knew she never would.

Jens pushed back his shoulders. He was done with this conversation, over feeling sorry for himself. He didn't whine or wail, he was someone who preferred action to introspection, doing to thinking. Why he'd even told Maja this much, he had no idea. They'd had sex, great sex, sure, but good sex wasn't a reason to spill his secrets. If it was, then he would've blabbed to several women who'd shared his bed over the years.

Jens felt irritated with himself. He stood up, injecting steel into his spine as he did so. 'I'm going for a run,' he coldly informed Maja, irked by the empathetic expression on her admittedly lovely face. He didn't need it. He didn't need *anything* from her.

She surprised him by nodding. 'I think that's a good idea. You need space and I probably could do with some too.'

He started to ask her why she needed space from him, then remembered that he was trying to put some emotional distance between them. And he'd succeeded. So why did he suddenly feel as if he wanted to reel her back in, stop her from going anywhere?

'Have something to eat, don't wait for me,' he said. 'If you want anything else, just call Reception. Then get some sleep. We'll be heading back to Bergen first thing in the morning.'

He hated the way he sounded. So cold. But better that than whining to the woman he was blackmailing into marrying him, about his mummy issues. He'd known that sleeping with her would be a bad idea, that it would add a layer of confusion to an already chaotic situation. He'd steamed ahead regardless.

He should've stayed sensible, resisted temptation and kept his trousers zipped.

* * *

Maja heard Jens move into the bedroom of the spectacular suite and her soft curses danced on the scented night air. She was horrified by his mother's actions, and a little hurt that he'd never told her any of this when they were together.

Maja pushed her self-pity away. This wasn't about her. She dropped her legs, let her bare toes touch the slate tiles and gripped the edge of the swing with both hands. His mother, and her refusal to let him be part of her life, hurt Jens badly. She now understood, on a deeper level than before, why he'd loathed their secret relationship. He would've thought she was embarrassed to be seen with him when she'd only been trying to protect him from her father.

But, in hindsight and with this new information, her insistence on secrecy would've been salt in his emotional wounds, her words a reminder of his mother and her rejection of him. Maja bit down hard on her lip and scrunched her eyes. Regret, hot and acid, swept through her. Had she known...

She couldn't change how she'd acted, but she could tell him the real reasons why she'd left, the part Håkon had played in her leaving. She had no idea whether anything she said would change his mind about her and the past, but he needed to know. She was sick of half-truths, lies and misunderstandings. How could they go forward if their foundation was built on shifting sands? But was she sure she wanted to go forward? With him?

Could she start again with Jens, meet him on level ground, see if they could resurrect a relationship from the scorched ruins of the past?

His hard exterior was a shell, and his sharp tone and cutting words were his way to keep the world at a distance. That wasn't who he was…she could see that now. Under his armour was the grown-up version of the man she once loved. A man who wanted to be acknowledged, loved, but was afraid of being rejected. Just as his mother had rejected him, just as Maja herself had. Or was she kidding herself? Did she want to believe he was better than he was because she was besotted by his body, entranced by the way he made her feel?

Jens appeared in the doorway to the suite, his face a thundercloud. 'I didn't bring any running shoes.'

She clocked his glittering eyes, the frustration on his face. He always used physical exercise to relax and to calm his washing-machine mind. He reminded her of a caged cat, a panther or a cougar about to jump out of its skin.

Maja lifted her thumb to her mouth, flicking her nail against her front tooth. She wanted to talk to him, explain why she left him and why she never returned. But when his eyes slammed into hers, she knew he wasn't ready to listen, wasn't in the right state of mind to hear anything she had to say.

He was frustrated, tense and probably regretting telling her about his mum. He wasn't a guy who wore his heart on his sleeve… Even twelve years ago, he'd kept his emotions under wraps. She'd known he'd loved her, but expressing his emotions wasn't something he'd known how to do.

Judging by the frustration pouring off him, he still hadn't fully learned that skill. For Jens, it had been, and was still, excruciatingly hard. And that was why he was left with a cauldron of bubbling emotions and nowhere to put them.

And if she pushed him to talk, he'd close down and retreat behind his thick wall of icy control. She knew that he'd get annoyed and he'd respond with cool indifference, all his arrogance on display, and they'd retreat to their lonely corners snapping and snarling. She didn't want to do that...

They could fight when they went back to Bergen. That wasn't what either of them needed now...

And if talking was out, then there was only one way to reach him, to help him. So Maja reached for the knot on her gown and pulled it apart, allowing the gown to drop from her shoulders onto the slate floor behind her. She'd pulled on matching underwear earlier, midnight-black panties and a matching low-cut bra. She pulled the band from her hair and her hair tumbled down her back.

She watched Jens swallow, his eyes travelling up her naked body, painting streaks of heat over her skin.

'Is sex your way of patting me on the head to make me feel better?' he growled.

She held his eyes. 'If you're going to be a jerk, then I'm going to go inside and go to bed. Alone,' she added, her voice pointed. He looked away and rubbed the back of his neck, a little flustered.

When he lifted his head, she saw lust in his eyes, but couldn't help but notice the determined set to his jaw, the tension in his mouth. He hated being on the back foot, not being in complete control.

He stalked over to her and gripped her jaw, his expression tough but his fingers gentle. 'This is just sex, Maja. Nothing more.'

He needed to think that. It made him feel as if he had a handle on the situation. Maja didn't know what was happening to them, where they were going or how they were going to get there, but she knew, with absolute certainty, that this was more than sex, more than two bodies bumping.

He'd get there...hopefully.

'When we get back to Bergen, things will be different,' he insisted.

Was he telling her or himself? Maja wondered.

Those dark blue eyes narrowed, and he looked like the predator he was. The back of his hand skimmed over her breast and the corner of his mouth hitched when her nipple pebbled against the lace of her bra. Her skin flushed pink. He lightly pinched her nipple and lust skittered through her, a bolt of dark energy.

'But I will take what you are offering, Maja.'

CHAPTER NINE

WITH THOSE LOW, heat-soaked words, Jens, carrying the wine bottle and two glasses, led Maja over to the far side of the wooden deck, where the magical half-light bounced off the bubbles of the hot tub sitting on the edge of the deck, suspended over the water-covered rocks below them.

Maja kept her eyes on his face as his hand drifted over her hip and around her back to find the clasp of her bra. It fell to the floor, draped over her bare feet. She tipped her head to the side as she watched him. His openly appreciative gaze heated, and she welcomed the familiar throb between her legs, the ache in her breasts. She wanted him to touch her but knew he'd ignore any demands to hurry things along. Jens wasn't in the mood to take orders...

Then again, he never was. And never did.

Jens half filled their glasses and left them sitting on the edge of the hot tub. His finger skated over her shoulder, across her collarbone, down to the swell of her left breast. He touched her as if this were the first time, as if he were learning her shape and textures all over again.

Maja gasped as Jens's finger brushed over her nipple. It tightened under his light touch. It was only one finger on one nipple and she was climbing, burning. And yearning for more. Would anyone ever make her feel like this again? Was it fair to expect anyone to? Would she ever be able to be with anyone but Jens again? She didn't think so.

She had the horrible feeling that after their time together was done—however long that might be and despite his stupid blackmail attempt—Jens would always have her heart. She'd given it to him twelve years ago...

He was intense, sharp, abrasive, he could be brutal. But she craved him...

Jens's breath skimmed over her cheek and his words landed lightly on her skin. 'Stop thinking,' he murmured. 'You don't need to do anything but feel what I do to you. Just be in the moment, open your senses. Feel my finger on your breast, taste my breath, and hear the sound of the water.'

Jens ran his finger down each bump of her spine, sliding it under the band of her panties, from her back to her front. He hadn't even kissed her yet and she was already wet, throbbing, desperate for him to touch her intimately, to fill her. This was supposed to be about him, but she was the one in need of more.

'Kiss me, Jens. Kiss me and then take me,' Maja said against his cheekbone.

'I'm too hard already and I'll only last three seconds if I do that.' To prove his point, Jens took her hand and placed it on his erection and Maja sucked in her breath. Her fingers drifted down the long, rock-hard length of him. He was so strong, so masculine.

Jens grabbed her wrist and gently, reluctantly, pulled her hand away and lifted his hand to tip her chin. She fell into the deep blue furnace in his eyes, her body on fire.

Maja moved closer to him, her breasts flirting with the cotton of his shirt. Jens encircled her hips with one arm and yanked her into him. Her stomach slammed into his hard erection and his tongue swept into her mouth. He tangled and teased her, his hand on the back of her head changing the angle of their kiss to discover another part of her mouth. His other hand slid beneath her black silk panties, and covered most of her butt. He went lower, then hoisted up the edges of her panties so he could stroke the tender skin of her inner thighs, allowing his fingertips to dance over her feminine folds.

He had too many clothes on, and she craved her hands on his bare skin. Maja shuddered as she found and undid his shirt buttons, breaking off the last one because she needed to have his broad chest and his hard, ribbed stomach under her fingers.

'Jens... Jensen...this...you...' she said, unable to form a complete sentence. Instead of talking, she stood on the tips of her toes to run her tongue along the underside of his jaw, to nibble on the cords of his strong neck.

Frustrated, needing him, she looked up to find his eyes on her face. All the air rushed from her lungs, and she desperately wanted to ask him what he was thinking. How much did he love this? What did he feel for her? Did he need her as she needed him? Was there more between them than a blackmail attempt, heartbreak and desire? She started to ask, then chickened out, knowing that words would only get in the way.

She would let their bodies talk and, at this point, they had a lot to say. She had just one, rather salient point, in her opinion, to verbalise. 'Jens, if you don't touch me soon, I'm going to scream from frustration. With volume.'

Jens looked down at her, a dark-haired Viking in complete control of himself and his surroundings. 'Go for it. Nobody is going to hear you.'

His thumb caressed her nipple, just briefly, before he pulled away. Maja groaned, as loudly as she could.

'You're killing me here, Nilsen,' she told him.

Jens turned away from her and stepped closer to the hot tub, bending to drag his hand through the water. Maja knew this image of Jens, bare-chested, his dark shorts hanging off his hips, looking at her with lust in his eyes, would be one she'd never forget. 'Take off your panties, Maja,' he told her.

He'd always taken charge in the bedroom but today there was an extra note of command in his voice. Whether it was an affront to her independence or not, Maja didn't know and didn't care. His bossiness in bed turned her on, so she slipped her thumbs under the band of her silk panties and pushed them down her hips. She kicked them away and waited for his next order.

He was a man with a plan, and she couldn't wait for it to unfold. It was deliciously intoxicating to hand over complete control. Her heart couldn't pump any faster, her lungs were unable to pull in more air.

Jens nodded to the hot tub. 'Hop in and sit on the edge of the hot tub.'

Maja took his hand and stepped into the hot, sweet-smelling water, immediately ducking her head under. She popped out, smoothing her wet hair back from her face.

'You look like a sexy mermaid,' Jens told her, but didn't

make a move to join her in the tub. But, judging by the action in his trousers, he was paying attention. A *lot* of attention.

'One minute,' Jens told her. He left her sitting on the edge of the tub and walked into the suite. She tipped her face to the fading sun, enjoying the silky air and the still-light night. She heard his footsteps and her eyes widened when she noticed the navy and black cotton scarf he held in his hand. It was one of hers. She'd worn it on her trip to Bergen a couple of days ago. He held it up. 'Do you trust me, Maja?'

She nodded. Yes, she absolutely did. Jens walked over to where she sat and kissed her shoulder.

Could a person die from being so turned on? Jens tied the scarf around her head, blocking the bright sunlight. 'Being deprived of your vision heightens all your other senses. Have a sip of wine and tell me if it tastes better with your eyes closed.'

When the glass touched her bottom lip, she placed her hands over his and took a sip, letting the liquid rest on her tongue before swallowing. 'It's deeper, mellower.'

'Does the water splashing the rocks sound louder? Is the night softer?'

Maja tipped her head to the side and nodded. The water swished over a rock and released a slight hiss as it pulled back. Then she heard the rustle of clothes hitting the floor.

Maja didn't know where Jens was until she felt his wet hands on the tops of her thighs, gently widening her legs. He was in the hot tub in front of her and Maja blushed. 'No, don't close your legs, Maja.' His voice caressed her bare skin, igniting baby fireworks on every inch. 'You are so very pretty, everywhere.'

Maja gripped the edge of the tub, her head tipped back, feeling uninhibited and free, as wild and untameable as the wild land surrounding them. Time ticked by, as sluggish as the blood moving through her system, as warm and thick as hot molasses. Seconds and minutes held no meaning, all that mattered was Jens's hands on her legs, what he was about to do to her and then, later, with her.

She could stay here for ever...

Maja jerked as his mouth, a little rough, a lot hot, wildly experienced, covered her sex and she arched her hips.

Maja whipped her head back and forth and Jens pleasured her, first with his lips, and then with his tongue. Then his fingers joined in, and he slid one finger into her, then two. Her orgasm built, a star about to explode, but just as she was about to let go he pulled back, and she thumped his shoulder with her fist.

'I asked you to trust me, Maja. I promise you I'm going to give you everything, all that you need. And more.'

He repeated the sweet torture, keeping her on the edge of pain-tinged pleasure but then he reached up and ripped the scarf off before his eyes slammed into hers. With his fingers still inside her, and his thumb on her clitoris, he leaned forward and whispered his order against her lips. 'Let go for me. Now.'

Maja screamed and dug her fingernails into his shoulders, now a shooting star streaking through the Milky Way. Despite the force of her orgasm, she needed more, she still felt incomplete. Slipping off the edge, she moved into the tub, causing warm water to slosh over the side and sending Jens's wine glass crashing to the deck. Neither of them cared. All that was important was to have him inside her, to ride another star again.

Maja wrapped her legs around his hips and Jens banded his arm around her waist, his mouth seeking hers in a kiss that was one part desperation, three parts fully turned-on male as she rode him.

Watching him, she saw his eyelids fall a little, the muscle in his jaw tense and his mouth flatten. He was holding himself in check, but she wanted him wild and out of control. Maja pushed her hand between them to take him in her hand, her thumb caressing his tip. He groaned and rested his forehead against her collarbone, every muscle in his body rigid.

'I can't tell you how much I want you, Maja.'

His voice was barely a whisper, the words dragged up from the depths of his soul. Maja felt powerful, a goddess, ruler of all she saw. This man, and her power over him, made her feel invincible.

Jens pushed into her, just a little. 'You feel amazing.' He lifted his hand and combed his fingers through the strands of her wet hair.

He surged into her, filling her up, as deep as he could go. 'So, so good,' he muttered.

He felt better, wonderful…amazing. She gasped when he lunged up and into her, hitting a spot she didn't know existed, one that sent tremors through her body.

She needed to hold off, just for a few seconds. Just long enough to lean back and wait for him to look at her, for those dark eyes to burn into hers. She touched his jaw with the tips of her fingers and brushed her thumb over his sexy bottom lip. 'Jens?'

'Mmm?'

'Let go. Do it…now.'

And, with a roar that was as primordial as their surroundings, Jens did as she ordered.

When she was sure Jens was asleep, Maja slipped out of bed and reached for his white shirt and slipped it over her head It fell to mid thigh and the sleeves dangled past her wrists. Turning the cuffs back, she tiptoed out of the bedroom, navigated the furniture in the sitting room and walked onto the secluded patio. On the swinging bench seat, she pulled her heels onto the cushion and wrapped her arms around her bent legs, her eyes on the mountains and the fjord.

She wished she could sit here and soak up the view in the magical light of a Norwegian summer night, but she needed to think, to work through the events of the past few days. Tomorrow they'd be leaving for Bergen and their truce, or whatever these past two days had been, would be over.

She had no idea what would happen when they returned to the Bentzen estate…would Jens cancel the wedding and agree to let her go? Would he still insist on them marrying? Had anything they'd said or done lately made any impression on him?

Jens was so impassive, utterly unreadable, and extracting any information from him was like trying to pull blood from a stone. He took being the strong and silent type to ridiculous lengths. She was still surprised he'd told her about his mum, given her that much information. Did he realise that she now knew his biggest secret? That she could use the information about his mum to blackmail her way out of being blackmailed?

She could demand that he cancel the wedding, and if he didn't, she could tell the tabloids Flora was his mum. But that would require proof and she had none. And, besides, there was no way she'd do that to Jens.

Maja sighed. Despite his few words on the subject, she'd heard the pain in his voice, and knew his mum's desertion was a deep and unhealed wound.

Up until today she'd never understood how their clandestine relationship had impacted him. Being a secret would've burned him every day, in every way, and would've deepened the emotional cuts inflicted by his mother.

If she'd had the smallest inkling of what his mother did, if she'd known about her refusal to acknowledge him, if she'd even suspected he had deep-seated issues about being thought of as a secret, she would've found another way, done things differently.

Maja clenched her fists and raised them to her temples. What would she have done differently? What other options had been available to her? Would she have had the courage to go up against her father? To put Jens, and his aunt, in financial danger? Would she have stayed, taken the chance? She had to be completely honest, she owed that to herself...probably not.

Because a part of her had been relieved to get that ultimatum from Håkon, a small slice of her soul had been looking for a reason to leave Jens and her father had handed it to her.

She'd loved Jens but she'd hated feeling like the lesser partner in their relationship. She'd adored him but had found herself frequently echoing his opinions, or going along with what he'd wanted, because she hadn't wanted to fight to be heard. She'd been besotted with him but had often felt overwhelmed by the force of his personality. She hadn't wanted to admit it, but he was an A-type personality, dynamic and strong-willed, so like her father.

Too much like her father.

But she was older now, stronger, and she wasn't the pushover she was when she was younger. She wasn't someone who just accepted what happened to her any more, she made her own luck, charted her own course. But she wasn't without her own arrogance; she'd thought she could sleep with Jens this time around and keep it surface-based... How wrong she was. From their first kiss she'd felt herself falling, sliding back into affection, maybe even love. Whatever she was feeling, she was in too deep. Her feelings for Jens—despite his stupid blackmail attempt—went far deeper than they should.

She could, maybe, possibly, be on the precipice of falling in love with him again.

But her feelings were her responsibility. She couldn't force Jens to feel more than he did. He loved her body, relished the sex, but that didn't mean he felt more for her than lust and desire. And that was...well, not okay, but she was old enough to know she couldn't force him to love her. Besides, there were still too many misunderstandings between them.

The one thing they could be was honest.

Jens's need for revenge was based on erroneous information. He only had part of the story of what had happened twelve years ago. She needed to tell him why she'd really left, shed light on her final days in Norway. If he knew the pressure she'd been under from Håkon, and if he knew her father had threatened to destroy Jens if they'd continued to see each other, maybe he would understand why she'd run. She'd been young, insecure, scared...he'd take that into account, surely.

Jens wouldn't keep blaming her for Håkon's actions after she left him. He wasn't an irrational man. If they could have an honest, open conversation they could sort this out, work through it. But twisting a steel rod was easier than getting Jens to talk.

But they were out of options and talking was something they needed to do before they found themselves in another situation, a marriage that would result in pain and misery.

The helicopter took off from the helipad at the Hotel Daniel-Jean and Jens looked back at Maja sitting behind the pilot. She wore a halter-neck navy-blue-and-white polka-dot dress, her bare shoulders more tanned than before. She'd pulled her hair into a ponytail and oversized sunglasses covered half her face. She looked fantastic, but then she always did.

He'd woken up this morning, found her side of the bed empty and went looking for her. He'd found her on the bench seat, her eyes on the mountain, deep in thought.

He'd recognised her expression, she'd been working something through, and he'd quietly retraced his steps, giving her space. In the shower he'd decided that, after an intense two days, backing away, creating some space, was an intelligent thing to do. And, if he had to judge by her muted response to his attempts at conversation over break-fast, she needed breathing space as much as he did.

Their 'time out' was done and he now had to plot a way forward and reassess their situation.

The flight to Bergen would take about an hour, so he had sixty minutes to decide which way to jump. Needing quiet, he pulled off his headset, making it impossible for the pilot or Maja to talk to him.

The question was simple…should they go back to how they were before, or did they need to find a new path forward? He'd told himself he wouldn't sleep with Maja, but that resolution went out the window when she asked him to take her to bed. He should've said no, but he was a man, not a monk, and no woman had ever turned him on quicker than Maja did.

But…*damn*. Making love to her was not just about a clash of body parts, a means to a blissful end. He couldn't forget he'd handed her his heart and she'd stomped on it. He was in danger of repeating old, very stupid mistakes.

He had a choice to back down, let her go or to continue with his plans for revenge. Could he cancel the wedding and watch her walk away and carry on with his life? Wouldn't that be an admission—silent or otherwise—that what she, and Håkon, did was okay? That leaving him with blithe, vague explanation via a breezy video was acceptable behaviour? His pride and self-respect wouldn't let that happen.

The second option was to cancel the wedding, ask her to stick around, to see whether they could have a relationship. What an absurd idea!

After she'd left, he'd stopped believing in relationships and emotional bonds, and he no longer required anyone's validation except his own. He was utterly self-sufficient, and he liked being that way. A second chance with Maja meant upending everything he believed in.

The easiest, most sensible and the safest option was to stick to his plan. The wedding invitations had been dispatched and their union was being touted as the wedding of the season. Cancelling it now would cause an uproar and media scrutiny would be intense. No, it was better for the wedding to go ahead...

But would he...could he still jilt her?

Jens looked down, barely noticing the lakes and fjords and the small villages far below them. He *had* to jilt her because, despite sleeping with her, he still favoured taking action over indulging in unproductive sentiment. He felt more comfortable with revenge than reconciliation.

As the pilot put more distance between them and Ålesund, as he flew him away from the romance of the fjords and the mountains, Jens's heart hardened. They'd shared two days, and they'd had great sex. She was still the reason Håkon had put a target on his back, and she was the one who had snapped his heart in two.

Nothing, really, had changed. Or that was what he was choosing to believe.

CHAPTER TEN

'I'LL SEE YOU in my office in fifteen minutes.'

Maja took the overnight bag Jens held out to her, caught off guard by his curt, cold tone. Before she could answer, he walked across the hall and disappeared into his home office, shutting the door behind him.

That one sentence was all he'd said to her since leaving Ålesund. They were back at the Bentzen Estate and Jens had reverted to being the impossible, remote, slightly supercilious man she'd met in the gallery a few weeks back.

Marvellous.

Maja looked down at the two overnight bags she held and frowned. Firstly, she wasn't Jens's butler, so she had no idea why he expected her to carry his bag to his room. And secondly, she wasn't quite sure where she was supposed to sleep now. In the guest room she'd occupied before she'd left for Ålesund, or in Jens's master suite? And if she was welcome in his private space, did she want to share it with him?

Maja placed his bag by his office door and carried her bag up the stairs. In the guest bedroom, she unpacked her clothes and freshened up. Through the open windows she heard the sound of a car on the driveway below. She pulled back the curtain and looked down onto the drive-way, frowning when she saw Hilda's Mercedes. Why was the wedding planner here? Had Jens called her? What was going on?

Maja left the bedroom and walked down the stairs. Jens was pulling the tall front door open.

'What's going on?' she asked him.

Jens didn't even bother to look at her, but greeted Hilda and ushered her into his study, brusquely ordering Maja to join them.

He gestured Hilda to a chair and walked around to sit in his expensive ergonomic chair behind his expansive desk. 'Forgive me for not offering you coffee, Hilda, but I'm way behind schedule.'

Hilda pulled her tablet out of her bag and nodded. She pulled the e-pen from its holder, poised to take notes. 'Please, go ahead, I'm listening.'

Jens tapped his index finger on the closed lid of his laptop. 'The wedding will be at the Hotel Daniel-Jean, two weeks on Saturday. I will pay the deposit as soon as we are done here.'

Hilda smiled, her budgie-like head nodding. 'Perfect. I think that will work—'

'What other information do you need?' Jens cut her off. He was back to being the cold, impersonal, bolshy billion-aire and Maja didn't like this version of him. And before they went any further, before they made any more deci-sions, she needed to talk to him, to tell him why she'd left, and what role her father had played in their break-up.

Until he had all the facts, they couldn't make any more

life-changing decisions. And getting married was a damn big deal.

'Jens, can I talk to you?'

His navy eyes connected with hers for a fraction of a second before he transferred his attention back to Hilda. 'Maja will take you into the smaller of the two sitting rooms and she will spend as much time as she needs to make the process of organising the wedding as easy as possible.'

Maja's eyes widened in shock. *What?* Why was he acting as if she were a wind-up doll? 'Hold on a second—'

'Maja, I need to work, and Hilda needs direction for a wedding that will take place in a fortnight. Decisions need to be made. *Today.*' Jens didn't give her a chance to respond but turned back to Hilda. 'Can you spend the rest of the day with Maja?'

'It would be my pleasure.' Hilda nodded, her expression enthusiastic.

Maja would rather poke hot sticks into her eyes. But she recognised Jens's determination, and knew that once Hilda got hold of her, there would be no escape. She'd had enough conversations with the wedding planner to know what questions she'd ask so she decided to condense hours of boredom and annoyance into a few sentences. Then Hilda could go, and she could tackle Jens.

'Shades of cream and white for the flowers, roses, and peonies. Soft and luscious arrangements. A string quartet playing before and directly after the ceremony, a live band for the reception. A blueberry buttermilk cake with a blueberry jam filling for the wedding cake, lemon for the groom's cake. What else?'

'The colour scheme?'

'I told you,' Maja replied, a little impatiently. 'Soft whites and cream, maybe with hints of a fresh green. Romantic and elegant.'

Hilda nodded, writing furiously. 'I can have mood boards done within—'

Maja waved her words away. 'Jens is paying you a fortune to get this done. I trust your taste.'

'What about your wedding dress, your attendants' dresses?' Hilda asked.

Maja closed her eyes and counted. She was *this* close to screaming. 'I'll sort that out.' She wasn't having bridesmaids. If she had her way, and she intended to, there would be no wedding. She was only answering Hilda's questions to get her out of the room so she could talk to Jens.

'Do you have enough to work on for now?' Maja asked her, praying she said yes.

Hilda stared at her tablet and finally nodded. 'I might have questions—'

'You have my phone number,' Maja assured her. To make sure that Hilda got the hint, she walked over to where she sat and picked up her bag. Hilda looked at Jens, and when he didn't say anything, she stood up and took her bag from Maja.

She slid her bag over her shoulder and told them she would be in touch. When Maja heard the front door close, she sat down in the seat Hilda had vacated and fixed her eyes on her fiancé's hard face. 'You and I need to talk.'

Jens gestured to his still closed computer. 'I have work to do, Maja.'

She tipped her head to the side. 'I think you misunderstood me, Jens. That wasn't a request.'

Some events and conversations were turning points in a person's life and Maja knew that whatever happened next would impact the rest of her life.

This was it, a come-to-the-light conversation with huge consequences. The urge to run was strong. She and Jens had to navigate the future and find a way to deal with each other going forward.

Maja shifted in her chair, crossed her legs and noticed her shaking hands. How would their conversation go? Would they fight? Be reasonable? Would they be able to find a way forward that didn't involve blackmail and marriage?

And would she know, at the end of the conversation, how much of the young man she loved remained, whether he was truly like her father and who Jens really was?

She'd seen flashes of the old Jens on the yacht and in Ålesund, had caught glimpses of the young man she'd known and loved. Jens could be funny and lovely, thoughtful and relaxed, the antithesis of the hard man in front of her. Bergen Jens was too like her father, hard, tough, abrasive and demanding. Those elements of his personality had scared her as a young girl, and she hadn't known how to handle them. Or him.

But she was an adult now, and better able to handle his domineering streak. She wasn't a wilting flower who'd crumble at a harsh word. She could stand up for herself, fight her corner, and wouldn't let herself be pushed around. She could handle Jens Nilsen.

Maybe.

Jens rested his forearms on his desk and his intense, irritated blue eyes met hers. 'Say what's on your mind so that I can get back to work, Maja.'

He didn't dance around the subject, and she was grateful.

Maja scooted to the edge of the seat and cupped her knee with her linked hands. After a minute of discarding one opening sentence for another, she settled on: 'You need to know why I left twelve years ago.'

His expression hardened. 'You said everything you needed to in that video, Maja. I don't see the point of raking through old history.'

He couldn't sound more uninterested if he tried. But behind the boredom, his 'couldn't care less' expression, she saw a spark of curiosity in his eyes and decided to push on. 'I left because it was the only way I could protect you.'

'What are you talking about? Protect me from whom?' Jens demanded.

'From Håkon,' Maja replied. 'The reason I didn't tell him about us, tell anyone, is that I didn't want him finding out about you until we were married. I needed Håkon in a position where he was forced to accept you, where he had to welcome you into his world. But he found out about you, and us, the week before, and I had no choice but to leave.'

'Hold on! Are saying Håkon forced you to leave me?' Jens demanded. Was that shock in his voice? It was hard to tell.

'Yes, he's why I left.'

'Explain, Maja.'

Maja decided not to call him on his bossiness. There were too many misunderstandings between them, and they needed to clear the air. They didn't need to fight about his high-handed attitude as well.

But she couldn't help her 'don't test me' glare. 'Håkon insisted I stop all contact with you.'

'Why? Because you were his princess?'

Maja snorted. 'I wasn't. What Håkon wanted was a son.' Was that really her voice? It held all the weariness of an old, out-of-tune piano. 'My mum nearly died when she had me and the doctors said it was dangerous for her to have more. Håkon pushed, determined to have his son. She resisted for a decade then, worn out by his persistent nagging, she fell pregnant again. She lost that baby, another girl.'

'You never told me that.'

They'd both kept parts of themselves hidden. 'I became a symbol of his failure, the unwanted girl child,' she added. 'Håkon disliked me but he needed control over me and what I did. I was, after all, a Hagen.'

He didn't speak so she carried on with her explanation. 'Anyway, after he found out about us, he told me that if I didn't cut off all contact with you, he'd sink your business, and make sure you never worked in the industry again. I didn't want that happening to you, so I ran.'

He stared at her. 'Maja, he did that anyway.'

What? She frowned. 'What do you mean?'

'Why do you think we've been feuding for the past twelve years?' Jens half shouted. 'He made it his mission to destroy me. Did you think our feud came out of nowhere?'

Her mind was a tumbleweed racing across a desert. 'He started it?' Of course, he did, it was vintage Håkon. Maja stood up, walked around to stand behind her chair and gripped its back. 'He said that if I went back to you, he'd buy out the leases on your boats, your fishing quotas, buy the building Jane lived in and evict her. But he did that anyway, didn't he?'

'He tried, but we came through it okay.'

She looked at him, thinking that he'd done better than okay. He'd become the only man who could match Håkon dollar for dollar, ruthlessness for ruthlessness.

'Why didn't you come to me?' Jens asked.

'I couldn't. He insisted on the video and watched as I sent it to you. I didn't feel like I had any other option than to do what he wanted.' Maja linked her fingers together and squeezed. 'I knew how powerful he was, Jens, and I wanted to protect you.'

Did he understand that? Was she getting her point across?

'Protecting me wasn't your job,' he snapped. He stood up and leaned his shoulder against the wall and looked out onto the landscape gardens beyond his window. It was such a stunning day and they were inside, arguing.

Then Jens, very deliberately, started to clap. Maja stared at him, and spread her hands, confused.

'Oh, kudos to Håkon,' Jens stated, his eyes now a bitter blue. He dropped his hands and shook his head. 'He outplayed, out-manipulated and outmanoeuvred me, the cantankerous bastard. I wasted twelve years because he wanted to play God. Well played, the son of a bitch.'

Jens had thought he knew what anger was, but the rage swirling through his system was more powerful than anything he'd experienced before. He fought the urge to plough his hand into the wall, to overturn his desk. He wouldn't, he was still in control. Just. But he did take a few moments to indulge in imagining how good it would feel to lose his temper, how satisfying it would be to throw his art deco lamp into the far wall, to launch his chair through the window.

But instead of losing his temper, he bunched his fists, his short fingernails digging into the skin on his palms. His jaw was tense enough to crack teeth and white-hot rage threatened to blister his skin.

Twelve years, wasted. He'd spent so much energy, and lost sleep cursing her. He was furious with Håkon, with Maja, with himself...

He also felt like an idiot, and that added another layer of rage.

It was so much to take in, too much to work through. A part of Jens wished Maja had kept this to herself, the rest of him struggled to make sense of the fact that Maja never, really, betrayed him. She'd left him, misguided as it was, to protect him. And in telling him that, she upended his world and turned it inside out.

This was the emotional equivalent of standing under a shower of boiling water, each droplet stripping a few millimetres of skin.

Jens couldn't look at her, not yet. He needed time to make sense of what she'd said, the past. Out of the corner of his eyes he saw Maja rock on her heels, looking unsure as to what came next. He was too, although he'd never admit that. He'd learned that when he felt off balance and weakened, it was best to say nothing.

He heard Maja murmur, 'Jens, please talk to me.'

He couldn't, not yet. If he did, he would make this situation worse. And it was horrible enough already.

He turned to look at her straight on, and inwardly

winced. She'd never been able, fully, to hide what she felt for him. All her emotions passed through her eyes. Under the layers of confusion, he saw affection, desire and the need to understand, and be understood. The need for connection. It was obvious that she wanted more from him, far more than he could give. He saw her hope that they could get through this, her desire for a reset, or a completely new start. Jens didn't know if she loved him, but he recognised the emotion jumping in and out of her eyes and across her face. She was in too deep...

Was he?

Maybe. But it didn't matter whether he was or not, he couldn't go there. Too much emotion caused complications, rewired the brain, and turned simple situations into chaos. She'd just stripped away the foundation for his revenge and he didn't know how to process the fact that she hadn't abandoned him all those years ago. He hated this churning feeling, his lurching stomach, the hitch in his breath. Feeling foolish and feeble, and insecure. He felt as he had when he was a child and that was wholly unacceptable. He hadn't worked every hour of the day for twelve years, built up a massive empire, commanded respect, to allow Maja, and his past, to destroy his sense of self-worth.

When faced with a fight, he didn't buckle or bend, he came out swinging. He never went down, and if and when he did, it wouldn't be without a fight.

He knew how to handle anger...so he embraced it, let it fuel him. His spine straightened and he lifted his chin and narrowed his eyes. If she wanted a conversation, she would get it. But he knew she wouldn't like it.

Game, he decided, on.

* * *

Maja had genuinely thought that having the truth of their break-up out there would allow them to move on, allow Jens to disregard his need for revenge. Her explanation had initially rocked him, but then his emotional shutters had dropped and she was on the outside trying to find a way in. He looked hard, emotionless, expressionless.

And why did she sense he was about to drop another conversational hand grenade? Something still didn't make sense between them, and she knew whatever it was was going to rock her world.

She didn't want to hear it, she wanted to go forward, blissfully ignorant.

'Can we just draw a line under everything, Jens?' she asked, sounding a little desperate. 'Can't we just give each other a blanket forgiveness for everything we did in the past?'

Jens's eyes slammed into hers and she knew he wouldn't allow her to duck out now. Whatever he needed to confess clearly burned inside him. He couldn't *wait* to tell her. She narrowed her eyes. *Why?*

'I never explained my reasoning for wanting to marry you, Maja.'

She frowned. 'You wanted revenge by making me fulfil my promise to marry you.'

Jens didn't drop his hard blue eyes from hers. 'You're half right. I also wanted to marry you so that I could leave you at the altar, just like you left me.'

His words dropped but it took Maja a minute to make sense of them. No! Nobody would go to such lengths, put themselves to so much trouble and expense, to get pay-back. Would they?

'You are not being serious, right?' She felt dizzy and spacy, as if her world were spinning far too fast.

Jens placed his hands flat against the surface of his desk. 'I blackmailed you into marriage so that I could leave you at the altar. I believed, *believe*, in an eye-for-an-eye type of revenge.'

But their circumstances were very different this time around. Twelve years ago nobody had known their plans to marry, and their break-up had been completely private. This time around, Jens had hired a wedding planner to throw a huge wedding in front of five hundred high-profile guests and planned on leaving her standing at the altar, alone. She would've been the laughing stock of Norway, of Europe, the lead headline in every publication around the world. Maja Hagen dumped by billionaire.

She'd known his intentions were, at best, suspect, but to take her on this ride simply to embarrass her publicly? Why would he do that? What would he gain from hurting her that way?

Revenge—against her, against her father—was more important than her feelings. That was the simple answer.

Her father would've done the same, he'd been a master of finding the punishment, or humiliation, to fit the crime. Jens had followed his example.

All her old doubts came roaring back, as hard and hot as before. She'd wanted a reset, to try and have a grown-up relationship with Jens, but how could she trust him? How could she give everything of herself to him, knowing he had the same ruthless streak her father possessed running inside him? What if she—or their kids, if they had any together— some time in the future, made the wrong move, upset him in some way, and he reverted to this vengeful petty behaviour? How could she go forward knowing that, with Jens, she felt as if she stood on shifting sands? That his love for her would depend on whether she pleased him or not?

She could never take that chance, not again. She'd lost her father because she'd silently questioned his every action and had never been sure of his motives. Håkon had never respected her needs or safeguarded her emotional well-being. He'd never put her first.

Maja gripped the back of her chair and dropped her head, the memories of her father flooding her system. The school reports she brought home that were never opened, the father-daughter dances he never attended, him leaving her alone, night after night in their huge mansion, with only the TV or her laptop to keep her company.

From the age of ten she'd raised herself, believing herself to be a disappointment, unwanted and unneeded. Håkon had betrayed her over and over again… Jens would probably do the same. Even if she got over him wanting to marry her for revenge, how could she put her heart in the hands of a man who was so like her father? Would she ever feel truly safe with him? Or would she have to be helpful and perfect, constantly walking on eggshells to receive Jens's attention and love?

'What else is on your mind, Maja?'

She hated that he could read her so well. Should she tell him that she saw her father in him, that they were, occasionally and in certain situations, two peas in a pod? He wouldn't welcome being compared to her dad.

And if it hurt him, if it stung…well, then maybe he'd also feel as if he'd been slammed into an electric fence. She wanted to hurt him too.

She hesitated. 'They say that girls either fall in love with men who are exactly like their fathers, or they are the complete opposite. You and Håkon are so very much alike.'

Shock skittered across his face. 'I am not *anything* like your father!'

She'd thought he'd say that. 'You're smart, driven, passionate about your business and very ambitious. You don't suffer fools gladly and you have a vengeful streak a mile long,' Maja pointed out, her tone bitter. 'You have to come out on top, every time.'

He didn't look away. 'You're right, I do. I wouldn't have feuded with your father for twelve years if I wasn't determined to win.'

She couldn't do this any more. His need for control, his need to control her, would always be greater than his need to be happy. She'd left Norway because she didn't want to be controlled by Håkon, and she'd spent the last decade living by her own rules. Was keeping M J Slater's identity secret so important that she was prepared to let a man tell her what to do, to chart the course of her life? What had she been thinking? Had she been thinking at all? Maja felt embarrassed and furious, with Jens but mostly with herself. He couldn't have played this game without her participation.

Maja raised her hands, her palms facing forward. 'I'm done, Jens.'

Shock briefly skittered across his face. 'Meaning what, Maja?'

This was the most honest, most hurtful conversation they'd had, ever would have, but Maja knew it was better to be hurt by the truth than fooled by a lie.

'I love you, I always have, probably always will, but it's not enough. I can't be controlled, I *won't* be coerced or controlled. I wouldn't stand it from Håkon, and I certainly won't tolerate feeling like that with you.' Knowing she was on the edge of breaking down, Maja turned and walked away.

From the man she loved more than life itself. But this time, crucially, it was her choice to walk away. Hers. She was the captain of her own ship, the creator of her life.

She'd never give anyone, not even Jens, that power again.

CHAPTER ELEVEN

JENS STRODE INTO the lobby of The Thief, one of the coolest hotels in Oslo. The hotel, right on the water's edge, surrounded by cafes, amazing art galleries and fantastic restaurants, was one of his favourites places to meet colleagues and clients. He loved the modern artwork on its walls and its stylish décor.

But he didn't notice any of that today. Since Maja had left him over a week ago, he couldn't shake off his irritability and anger. He'd failed in his quest to get revenge, to close the circle. He'd handled Maja badly, and it was galling to admit he'd lost control. He wasn't someone who tolerated failure, in others or in himself. He was jumpy and jittery, off balance and out of sorts.

He was resolved to call off the wedding—his bride and his need for revenge were both gone—he just needed to instruct his PR person to draft the press release. But he had this need to understand *everything*, or as much as he could, before he made any irreversible decisions.

Because, in all honesty, his ability to make rational, sensible decisions seemed to have deserted him. And he was swamped by the need to go back to where it all started. His *issues* didn't start with Maja or Håkon. No, they went back further than that. If he was going to move forward, and he wanted to, he needed to understand his dysfunctional relationship, if thirty years of neglect could be called that, with his mother. It was time to put as many of his demons as he could to rest. He'd based his need for revenge on flawed reasoning, and he'd hurt Maja in the process. Before he could pick up the pieces of his life, he needed to make sure he had *all* the pieces of the puzzle. That meant going back to the start, to Flora, to see what he was missing.

It was fortuitous Flora was in Oslo to receive an award and it was common knowledge she was staying at The Thief. According to the hotel manager, a man Jens knew well, Flora was in her room, but she wasn't taking visitors. Jens asked him to dial her room number again, took the receiver from the manager. He introduced himself, told Flora he wasn't going away and that they could either speak in her room or he could wait for her in the lobby. Within a minute, he was in a lift heading for her floor. Flora, dressed in a silk trouser suit, opened the door to her suite. She didn't look pleased to see him. *Shocker.*

'What do you want?'

'You're back in Norway, for the first time in over thirty years,' Jens smoothly replied, although his heart was beating as fast as a hummingbird's wing. 'I thought we should chat.'

Flora motioned him into the suite and Jens took in the fine wrinkles make-up no longer covered, her hard blue eyes, and her tight mouth. She looked remote, ice cold and fully uninterested. Did people see the same dissatisfaction when they looked at him? Someone perpetually discontented by life, talented but emotionally empty?

'If you are here to beg me to acknowledge you, I won't,' Flora defiantly told him.

He started to respond then stopped, shocked as a missing puzzle piece dropped into its empty spot. He didn't need her to. Not any more. He no longer needed to be accepted by this miserable, empty-hearted woman. She'd had little to no input into his life, she hadn't given him anything but his looks and an inability to trust, his issues of abandonment. He didn't want to be like her, in any way. It was time to let her go. But if this was the last time he'd see her, he needed to make sure those demons would never rear their ugly heads again. He looked at the small, elegant woman and when his words left his mouth, he was surprised at how gentle he sounded. 'Why did you give me up?' he softly asked.

She sighed, her hand fiddling with her thick gold necklace. Flora walked over to the couch and sank into the plump cushions. Sitting down, she looked older, as if the world had chewed her up and spat her out. Was that how he would look when he was sixty, discontented and miserable?

Flora lifted a too thin shoulder. 'Jane wasn't particularly maternal,' she finally answered him, 'but I was far worse.'

Jens lifted his eyebrows, staying silent in the hope she'd continue. 'When I got the offer to go to New York, I knew I didn't love you enough to take you with me. In fairness, I didn't love anyone enough. I'm not capable of putting other people first, not really capable of loving anyone either.'

He was astounded by her honesty. But instead of her words hurting, he felt cleansed by them. It helped to know she would've dumped anyone she perceived to be a handbrake. Her leaving was all about her, not him. She was self-absorbed, probably narcissistic, deeply, comprehensively selfish. He got it. Flora was the problem, not him.

'Leaving you with Jane was the best thing I did for you, my one unselfish act,' Flora quietly stated, sounding old and weary. 'I couldn't be a good mother, any type of mother. I didn't have it in me. Jane did.'

Jens pondered her statement. She was right, handing him to Jane—straightforward but stable—had been the right thing to do. Flora had hurt him but she'd done what she'd thought was right for him. Maja had also acted in his best interests when she'd left him twelve years ago. Both situations had been painful but both women had done what they'd thought was right. How was it possible to feel hot, and cold, at the same time? Miserable but unburdened? Grateful that they both loved him, in diametrically opposite ways and situations. That they had put him first, no matter what it had cost them? He felt foolish, full of regret, but more like himself than ever before.

Flora tossed her deep brown curls. 'So are you going to go to the press or not?'

No, he didn't need to. Who would care and how would it change his life? Flora giving him to his aunt would be news for about five minutes and then everybody would move on, and the world would keep turning. And he'd already wasted too much energy on her. Sorting out his relationship with Maja would be a far better use of his time.

Jens sighed. For a hotshot businessman, a super-effective deal-maker, he'd made a series of miscalculations and errors in judgement. He might be able to swim through the shark-infested waters of international business, but he was unable to look at relationships clearly.

Was it any wonder, since he'd had so little practice? Because he'd been raised to be like his aunt, unemotional, he shied away from talking about his feelings. Maja was the only woman who'd managed to slide under his electric fence guarding his heart, then and now.

And yes, he was as much in love with her as he'd ever been. But, because he'd been consumed by revenge and the need to get even, to be acknowledged, to be seen to be the winner, he'd lost her before they'd even started. Jens felt a rush of emotion, of regret, and, instead of talking himself out of it, running from it, he squared his shoulders and faced his past.

Flora was Flora, uninterested in him, and he no longer cared. Maja, coerced by Håkon, had left her home, her country and broken ties with her father, all gutsy moves for a teenager and she'd done it to protect him. Maybe she could've chosen another route, acted differently, but she'd been eighteen, a kid.

It was also time for him to stop feuding, even if it was only in his own mind, with Håkon. The man was dead, for the love of God! He'd been pretty awful in life, hard and selfish, full of revenge and selfish to the core. Emotionally cold and uninterested. Inflexible, self-indulgent, controlling, spoiled, resentful, arrogant...

He fully understood why Maja thought he and Håkon were so alike. For all the reasons that Maja had said. Everything he'd hated about Håkon were the things he most disliked about himself. Jens wanted to look away, to move his thoughts on to something more pleasant, but he had to face himself. Everyone did at some point in their lives. He had a choice to make...

He could imitate Flora, be selfish and eschew relationships, and live his life in the semi-darkness of loneliness. Or he could fight for the light.

Most of that light was Maja. She brought joy and happiness into his life. He might have all the money he could need, enough for several lifetimes, have power and influence, and be praised and pandered to, but life without Maja meant nothing. And his obsession with revenge had cost him the only thing that had ever meant anything to him.

He needed another chance, a second chance, to be happy...to live and love and laugh. How could he convince her that he wanted her in his life, that she was all that was necessary for him to be happy?

He put his powers of critical thinking to amass his fortune, and to strike complicated deals. It was time to use those skills to get Maja to agree to marry him, to be his.

For as long as they both might live...

'Jens?'

Jens jerked his head up, remembering where he was and who he was with. Flora. *Right.* He walked over to her and placed a brief kiss on her cheek. It was the first time he'd touched her in over thirty years. And it would be the last. It was a brief hello, and a final goodbye. 'Congratulations on your award, Flora. Have a good life.'

Tension and discontentment drained from his system as he left his birth mother, and his past, in that stylish hotel room and walked towards his future.

Back in Edinburgh, after many sleepless nights, Maja stepped out onto the tiny balcony leading off her bedroom. Usually, her view of Edinburgh Castle always held her attention but lately her attention span was all over the place. She'd left the Bentzen estate after her confrontation with Jens and caught the next flight back home. She'd been back a week and was still trying to gather her shattered and battered heart together.

Maja rested her hip on the railing. While she loved Scotland, she couldn't help but acknowledge that she adored Norway. The country had seeped back into her pores, invaded her soul. There was still so much of it she wanted to rediscover, more of its natural wonders to admire. She loved the cobalt blues of the fjords, the verdant greens of the valleys, the purple and white mountains, and skies so endlessly clear it hurt her eyes. But how could she go back to Bergen? How could she live in a city that would for ever be filled with memories of Jens?

Maja yawned and took another sip of her strong black coffee. She should get back to learning her new photo-editing software, but she was getting nowhere. As best she could, she pushed any thoughts of Jens away, but, since she often found tears running down her face, she knew she needed to deal with finding him, loving him, and losing him again. Some things couldn't be avoided, and this was one of them.

But where to start? Maybe the answer was not to 'start' anywhere but to allow her thoughts free rein. Her thoughts tumbled over and over, and she watched them float by, concentrating on those that felt right, the ones that came through strongest.

That she was tired of secrets and sick of shadows was her first revelation. She had to come out from hiding behind her M J Slater pseudonym. She wouldn't have got into this mess with Jens in the first place if she hadn't been so hell-bent on protecting her pseudonym, if she hadn't been so against the world linking her art with her being Håkon's estranged daughter.

But she *was* his daughter, she *was* a Hagen. She couldn't run away from it any more. And she didn't want to. She might be Maja Hagen, but she was a separate entity from her father. If a couple of critics said she was trading off her last name, what did it matter? She had great reviews and a successful exhibition as M J Slater to counter those accusations. She knew the truth, she knew how hard she'd worked to get where she was. She always said she wanted her art to speak for itself and it did, it always would. It would speak no matter who signed her images. And she wanted to sign them as Maja Hagen…

Because Maja Hagen was the woman who'd left Norway, who'd made mistakes and struggled to find herself. What had started as a way to protect herself had become a limitation and she was done with limits. She'd used her art as a shield, and she hid behind it. And as long as she kept her identity a secret, she couldn't fully engage with anyone. Not with lovers, friends, or clients. It was a barrier, a way to keep her safe.

Maja Hagen was done with being safe, so she sent a text message to Halston.

Can you prepare a press release explaining that M J Slater is Maja Hagen?

Halston immediately replied.

Seriously?

Yes. Keep it simple and send it through to me for approval when it's done.

Now it was time to deal with her six-foot-something problem of loving Jensen Nilsen. What was she going to do about him? And even if he wanted a relationship with her—his silence said he didn't—could she ever trust him? If they got together and they hit a bump in the road, would their relationship survive the crash? They had the ability to hurt each other, in every way possible. Could he love her the way she needed him to?

She didn't think so. He'd planned to leave her at the altar, so caught up in his need for revenge that he was prepared to humiliate her on an industrial scale.

Jens had massive trust issues, ones she didn't think would ever go away. His mum had never acknowledged him. Maja had promised to marry him but had run out on him instead. Håkon had tried to destroy him. Why would he trust anyone?

Maja loved him, she always would. But love without trust was a car without an engine, a river with no water. Without trust, there was no reason to continue.

Maja placed her coffee cup on the table, her diamond ring flashing blue fire in the sunlight. She held the stone with her index finger and thumb, admiring the deep blue colour. It reminded her of Jens's eyes and the deep blue of the fjords. She'd have to give him the ring back. There was no way she could keep it. But that meant seeing him. She couldn't let a third party handle the transfer of such an expensive ring.

They'd have to meet at some point. She had clothes at his house, toiletries, and she wanted to know if she could have the art books in her grandmother's studio. They needed to end this chapter in a civil, sensible way. She couldn't run away again...

Maja heard someone trying to attract her attention and looked down to see a blonde bike courier on the pavement, a package in her hands. The courier looked up at her, squinting in the sun.

'Maja Hagen?' When Maja nodded, the biker told her she had a delivery.

Maja walked downstairs. She took the plastic envelope and ripped it open. Inside was a plain white, square envelope, with her name written across it in a bold black fountain pen. She recognised Jens's handwriting...

Her heart rate picked up. 'Do you need me to sign for it?' Maja asked, looking for a reason to delay opening the envelope. Jens was a direct guy, someone who didn't shy away from confrontation, and his sending her a paper and pen message couldn't be good.

The courier shook her head, walked away and Maja turned the envelope over, then over again. Back in her flat, she paced, putting the envelope down, and then picking it up. Finally, irritated by her actions, she ripped the envelope open and pulled out the thick, expensive invitation.

Jens Nilsen and Maja Hagen
invite you to join them
to celebrate their wedding
at the Hotel Daniel-Jean...

Maja frowned. Why would he send her a copy of their wedding invitation? Why hadn't he cancelled the wedding? What was he trying to say?

She flipped the card over. Jens had scrawled a sentence.
It took her a while for the words to make sense.

I'm going to be there. Are you? ·

CHAPTER TWELVE

THIS WAS THEIR wedding day and she was in the back of a taxi. Maja had flown into Ålesund hours ago and dressed in a bland hotel room and wondered if she was making the biggest mistake of her life. The taxi pulled up to the entrance of the Hotel Daniel-Jean and Maja laid her hand over her heart, telling it to calm down.

She was about to walk through the lobby, clutching a bouquet of white and cream roses, dressed in a simple but deliciously gorgeous wedding dress of French-lace-covered satin, her make-up and hair as good as she could get it...

And she didn't know if Jens would be waiting for her in the gazebo at the end of the pier. He could be playing with her, this could all be one huge set-up, his way to exact payback... Was this a mistake? Was she setting herself up for failure?

Maja looked over the shoulder of the driver to the clock on the dashboard. She was on time. She turned her head to the side and watched an elegant couple slip into the hotel, hurrying to be there before the bride. She resisted the urge to roll down the window and ask them to check whether a suited and booted groom was waiting for her.

Maja pushed her fist into her sternum and wondered, not

for the first or five thousandth time, what she was doing. There was a chance she was walking into more heartbreak, a press firestorm, a PR disaster. She'd just claimed her name back, and the art world was excited to discover the real identity of M J Slater. She was courting trouble with this stunt.

If Jens failed to appear, or walked away before they said 'I do', she'd be a headline tomorrow. She would be laughed at and commented on over morning coffee and marmalade on toast. She would be Norway's, maybe even Europe's, morning entertainment.

But, if Jens was there wanting to marry her, they would be extraordinarily happy, and her life would be complete. When she thought about it like that, there wasn't a chance she wouldn't take, a move she wouldn't make, to be with him. She loved him and, because she did, she'd do anything, risk anything, to have Jens in her life…

That didn't stop the butterflies in her stomach from whirring and buzzing. But she couldn't sit in this taxi, biting her lip. She needed to move, to face whatever lay beyond those impressive hotel doors.

Maja thanked the driver, opened the door and stepped out onto the driveway, shaking out the folds of her dress. She'd opted out of wearing a veil, deciding instead to thread a few luscious cream roses, touched at the edges with blush pink, into her twisted-back hair.

You can do this, Maja. You have to know.

She'd had the mantra on repeat but, now that she was facing a long, lonely walk to the gazebo where the ceremony was to take place, her knees felt a little soft. She would not stumble at this last hurdle. She would not run away. She had to see this through, she had to *know*...

There was such power in making decisions for herself, in having the freedom to chart her own course. She was taking a chance on Jens, risking her heart again. It felt wonderful, and terrifying. This could backfire horribly, but she knew if she didn't, she'd regret not being brave for the rest of her life. Jens deserved her bravery, and she owed it to herself.

Maja walked through the lobby onto the wide veranda of the hotel and looked down. Hilda's team had set up flower-decorated chairs, placing them in regimented rows on the lush lawn. The rows were bisected by a white carpet leading up to the stairs of the pier. Big screens on either side of the pier were there to transmit the ceremony to the guests. Maja stared into the shadows of the gazebo, conscious of her knocking knees and a pool of sweat gathering at the base of her spine.

She looked into the rose-festooned gazebo and her heart settled when she saw Jens standing by the simple altar, his hands clasped and his head down. He was there, waiting for her. He'd been prepared to take the risk of her not showing up, was willing to be vulnerable, and he'd put himself in a position to be humiliated...for her.

Maja understood, on a deep fundamental level, how much courage it took for him to do that, especially since he had no idea whether she'd arrive or not. This was Jens putting his heart on a plate. And what a gift it was. Maja placed her free hand on her heart and allowed her pretty bouquet to rest against her thigh.

As if sensing she'd arrived, Jens lifted his head, and across the swathe of lawn their eyes connected. His shoulders dropped and a small smile touched his mouth. None of their guests suspected how monumental this moment was, what they'd gone through to be here.

Maja lifted her bouquet and used her free hand to lift the hem of the dress off the floor to walk down the steps to the lawn, and onto the white carpet that would take her to the altar, and Jens.

He was everything, and the only thing, she needed.

'Maja…'

Maja stepped into the gazebo, and Jens was convinced his heart was about to fly out of his chest. She was here. *Finally.*

She used her bouquet to gesture to his clothes. 'I like your outfit, Nilsen.'

Getting ready for his wedding was a blur and, unable to remember how he looked, he stared down at his stone-coloured trousers, the matching waistcoat, blue tie and cream shirt. He'd rolled the sleeves up to his elbows. A perfect cream rose, just about to bloom, was pinned to his waistcoat.

'I prefer yours,' he told her, his voice hoarse. Maja wore a Boho-inspired dress with a deep V-neckline. Her make-up was minimal, her hair was in a casual twist, decorated with baby roses. She looked breath-stealingly beautiful.

'I wasn't sure whether you'd be here,' Maja admitted.

He'd been hanging around the gazebo for hours, hoping to see her arrive, his heart in his throat. 'Funny, I wasn't sure you'd—'

Jens heard the officiant clearing his throat and turned to look at him. He nodded to the guests and Jens remembered they had an audience. Their every word and gesture was being transmitted to the big screens outside.

Jens turned to the officiant. 'We need a few minutes,' he told him. He found the camera mounted amongst the roses on the roof of the gazebo and slashed his throat. He waited for the light on the camera to go from green to red. When it did and the priest left the gazebo, he knew they were alone. Jens placed his back to the guests, his big frame hiding Maja from them, and looked down at his fiancée, the woman he desperately wanted to be his wife.

'I told you I would be here,' Jens said.

He took her hand and placed it on his heart, which was beating far too fast, wondering if she understood what it took for him to wait for her, the risk he'd taken, how scared he was.

She thought he was tough, unemotional, but this past week had been hell. He'd had no idea if she'd show up or not or hand him another dose of rejection. He'd thought about reaching out to ask her but had known he couldn't. He needed to show her that he was prepared to risk his heart, risk feeling humiliated for her. Despite feeling uncomfortable and vulnerable, he would walk through the fires of hell to make her understand how much he loved her.

Did she realise she was all that mattered?

She gestured to his clothing and then tipped her head back to nod at the full church. 'So, are we doing this?' she asked, trying to sound brave.

He knew, instinctively, that his being here wasn't enough, that she needed more from him than to simply rock up. She needed words, big and bold.

He could only think of a few. 'I love you, *min kjære.*'

Her big smile, the one he wanted to see every day for the next sixty years, was brighter than the sun. 'I know.'

He tipped his head to the side. 'How?'

'Jens, I'm old enough to know that love isn't only smooth words and over-the-top gestures.' She took his hand and rubbed her thumb over his knuckles. 'Love can also be standing up in front of five hundred guests, making a silent but powerful statement that I am who you want. You wouldn't risk being jilted unless you loved me.'

She squeezed his hand. 'But you could've told me before and saved us both a lot of angst.'

He rocked on his feet. 'I know but I needed—'

'To do this? To make the big gesture? I get it.'

She did. She got him. Jens lifted his hand to grip her neck. He rested his forehead against hers. 'I'm so in love with you, Maja. And I'm so tired of being without you.' He hauled in a breath. 'I'm done living my life like this. I'm done with feeling empty. I'm done with making work my priority and treating sex and women as temporary pleasures, here today and gone tomorrow.

'I saw Flora,' he admitted.

She pulled back, shocked. 'You did?' *Wow.* 'Is she going to acknowledge you?'

He shook his head and Maja grimaced in sympathy. She thought he was disappointed, but he wasn't. 'We can talk more about this later, but I no longer need her to acknowledge me.'

Before she could comment on that bombshell, he spoke again. 'Maja, I need you to know that I don't want to marry you because you are Håkon's daughter. I'm done with revenge. You, and any children we have, will be my *only* priority,' Jens added. 'I will be a good husband and a good father, Maja.'

'I know you will, Jens.'

He had Maja exactly where he wanted her, in a white dress, standing at the altar, telling him she loved him, but it wasn't enough. He needed to give her more, to give her everything. And that meant putting their future in her hands. 'Are you sure that this, being here, is what you want to do, *min kjære*?'

Maja laughed as she gripped the material of Jens's shirt and twisted her fingers, pulling the fabric tight against his chest and him a little closer to her. 'Jensen Nilsen, are you determined to give me a heart attack?' she asked, a wide smile on her face.

Jens placed a kiss on her temple before pulling back, his hands on her bare shoulders, his expression sincere but determined. 'Don't get me wrong, I'm not going anywhere. You told me you love me so you're not getting rid of me now.'

Too right she wasn't!

Jens spoke before she could, his hand coming up to cradle her face, his thumb on her lower lip. 'I just don't want you to feel pressured into marrying me. I know the last two months have been crazy and maybe you need some time to make sense of everything. We don't *have* to get married.'

What rubbish! She knew exactly what she wanted, and she'd tell him if he'd just give her a chance to speak.

'I'm happy to go out there and tell everyone the wedding is off. We can go home, or to my *hytte*, anywhere you like, and talk it through,' Jens suggested. 'We can take as long as you need.'

She knew a way for them to be together, and it was pretty damn simple. 'Or we can get married, right here and right now,' she suggested, looking up at him.

Excitement and relief fought for dominance in his lively blue eyes. 'Are you sure?' he asked her, moving his hands to her hips. Maja was glad he held her as she wasn't sure she could stand upright on her own.

'I'm *positive*, Jens. I want you in my life. I've *always* wanted you in my life. From the moment I saw you, twelve years ago and in the gallery a few weeks ago, I knew you were the one.'

Jens untangled her fingers from his shirt to lay her palm flat on his chest, above his heart. Through the thin fabric, she picked up its rapid beat. 'I felt the same. My heart knew it, but my mind, and my pride, needed some time to catch up.'

She lifted an eyebrow. 'Some time?'

He half winced, half smiled. She met his eyes and, within those gorgeous navy-blue depths, saw her future. She wasn't alone any more. Jens was going to be with her every step of the way. He'd run the risk of being jilted and put himself in a vulnerable position for her. Then, after telling her he loved her, he loved her enough to step back, to give her time to think. He'd relinquished control, and that was such a big deal for Jens. That, more than anything else, reassured her.

'Uh…folks…?'

They both whipped around at the interruption. The priest stood at the entrance of the gazebo, his hands clasped behind him and his expression worried. Maja felt Jens's arm around her waist, and she leaned into him, happy to soak up his strength.

'Do we have a problem?' the priest asked gently. 'Because I have a congregation who needs to know whether to stay or to go.'

'Just a minute more,' Jens told him.

Jens opened his mouth to speak but Maja put her finger on his lips. 'My turn, darling.' She smiled, happiness rolling over her in warm waves. 'I love you.' She stroked his jaw with her thumb and shuddered with love-tinged desire. 'Will you marry me, right here and right now, Jensen?'

Jens covered her hand with his. 'It will be my absolute pleasure.'

He ducked his head to kiss her, then pulled back at the last moment, choosing to lay a long, open-mouthed kiss on the side of her mouth. 'No, the next time I kiss you, you'll be my wife.'

Jens loved her, they were going to get married, and they were each other's future. Right, what now? Should she stay here, or walk down the aisle again?

Luckily, her clear-minded, but equally happy-looking, fiancé took charge. He motioned to the priest to take his place, picked up the bouquet she hadn't realised she'd dropped, before straightening a rose behind her ear. 'Ready?' he gently asked her, his mouth quirking in that sexy smile.

Maja nodded. 'For you? For this? Absolutely.' She shook out her dress and stroked her hand down the bodice. 'Shall I walk down the aisle again?'

Jens smiled and shook his head. He took the hand he

held and pulled it under his muscled arm. 'No, just stay with me, side by side.'

Side by side…

For ever together. Starting right now.

EPILOGUE

MAJA LOOKED AT the huge image on the gallery wall in Soho and wrinkled her nose. She'd captured Ben, their two-year-old son, jumping in a rain puddle, his grin, so like his father's, as wide as the sun. The photograph, the only one of Ben she'd allow to be exhibited and definitely not for sale, was the inspiration for her current collection, called *Sunshine and Joy*.

It was the opening night of her first major exhibition since Bergen and she was as nervous as a shocked cat. She was convinced the critics would hate her photographs and nobody would buy anything. Maja was pretty sure she was going to be a one-hit wonder.

She turned to look at Jens, who stood by her side, his big hand rubbing her lower back. 'What was I thinking?' she demanded, keeping her voice low. 'Giving up my pseudonym, thinking I could exhibit again?'

'Relax, darling.'

Easy for him to say! Every one of her images, ranging from the photograph of two homeless people roaring with laughter, to an exceptionally old lady talking to her equally old dog, were ripe with emotion. The thread running through all the photographs was joy, something Maja had experienced a lot of over the past three years.

And because she was so happy, she was drawn to finding moments of happiness in her work. But happiness wasn't a good subject for an exhibition. Critics and curators preferred angst and despair, they made for better subjects.

'I should never have agreed to this,' Maja muttered, frowning. 'I told you it was a bad idea.'

Jens turned her to face him and lifted his hands to hold her face. He dropped a kiss on her mouth and she, as always, tasted his desire. It didn't matter that she was seven months pregnant with their second child, their sexual buzz never went away. He pushed a curl off her forehead, and she fell into the blue of his eyes. He loved her, so much.

She, and their children, one at the hotel with his beloved nanny, one on the way, were the reason his world turned. He kept a tight rein on his businesses, but often worked from home, taking frequent breaks to spend time with her or Ben, and to give her time in her darkroom or studio. When he did go into the office, he made sure he was home in time to bath Ben and put him to bed.

He was an amazing entrepreneur but an even better husband and father.

'*Min kjære*, the world has enough images of destruction and darkness. It needs images like yours.' He placed his hands on her shoulders and told her to look around the room. 'Look at the smiles, the way people look at your images and then look at them again. They want to fall into the world you've captured.'

He dropped a kiss on her temple and Maja's breath caught at the love she saw on his face. 'I'm the lucky guy who gets to live in your world, Maja. I am so grateful for that.'

She touched his jaw with her fingertips. 'It's our world, Jens.'

He shook his head. 'These photographs, they're all you. Our wonderful lives, our children, also all you. I can't imagine what my life would look like without you in it.'

She thought about their already rumbunctious son, loud and oh-so-busy, and knew that their second son, who'd make his appearance in a couple of months, would be as energetic. She placed a hand on her bump and grinned. 'It would be quieter, that's for sure,' she told him, laughing.

'I'll take noisy and busy and ridiculously happy over quiet and empty any day of the week,' Jens assured her. He looked over her shoulder and squeezed her hand. 'Esteemed art critic coming in.'

She nodded, pasted a smile on her face and squared her shoulders. This was what she'd wanted when she'd shed her M J Slater skin: to stand by her work. She could cope with someone criticising her work to her face. Maybe.

'Maja Hagen! Let's talk about your art...'

Before stepping back, Jens squeezed her hand and sent her a reassuring smile. 'You've got this,' he quietly told her.

Maja nodded. Yes, she had. As long as she had him, she had *everything*...

* * * * *

Did The Tycoon's Diamond Demand
have you enthralled?
Then don't miss these other dazzling stories
by Joss Wood!

The Twin Secret She Must Reveal
The Nights She Spent with the CEO
The Baby Behind Their Marriage Merger
Hired for the Billionaire's Secret Son
A Nine-Month Deal with Her Husband

Available now!